WHEN DREAMS *are* CALLING

CAROL VORVAIN

Published by Carol Vorvain in 2014
Copyright © Carol Vorvain 2014

This is a work of fiction. Names, characters, places and incidents either are the product of the author's imagination or are used fictitiously. Any resemblance to actual persons, living or dead, events or locales is entirely coincidental.

Visit carolvorvain.com to find out more about Carol Vorvain and her books. You will find extracts, pictures, author events and you can sign up for newsletters to be the first to hear about her latest releases and special offers.

Paperback ISBN: 978-973-0-16625-5

No Fear, No Courage
No Dreams, No Life

CONTENTS

PROLOGUE: WORDS HAVE POWER, DREAMS HAVE POWER,
WE HAVE POWER   1

PART ONE: THE WAKE-UP CALL

1   THE WORLD OF A DREAM CHASER   5
2   BUCHAREST: THE LITTLE PARIS   18
3   PUPPY LOVE   22
4   A CAREER: BETWEEN PASSION AND CHORE   28
5   DEPRESSION: AN OPPORTUNITY OR A CURSE   33
6   FAMILY IS FOREVER: HAZARD OR BLESSING   39
7   LEAVING THE LAND OF DRACULA   43

PART TWO: CANADA, LEARNING THE ART OF LIVING

8   THERE IS NO OTHER TRIP LIKE THE ONE WE
EMBARK ON FINDING OURSELVES   51
9   BEFORE JOBS, THERE ARE CHOICES   61
10   EDUCATION SHOULD NOT BE DENIED TO THE ONES
WHO WANT TO LEARN   66
11   A CHINESE ROOMMATE, THE PHILOSOPHY OF A
NATION   73
12   NIGHT WATCH AT A HOTEL, LOULOU - THE WILD
CHICKEN AND LINGERIE'S MYSTERIES   77
13   FRIENDSHIP AND ITS PERKS   87
14   WHEN KINDNESS DOES THE TRICK   95
15   A FEW GENUINE ADVANTAGES OF LIVING ALONE   99
16   CUBA: LA DOLCE VITA   103

17 PERU: MAN-MADE AND GOD-MADE ISLANDS   109

18 CHALLENGES, OUR OPPORTUNITY TO SHINE   117

19 WHY J'AIME LE CANADA   121

PART THREE: AUSTRALIA, LIVING THE LIFE OF MY DREAMS

20 MELBOURNE: FOOTIE AND SCHIZOPHRENIC
    WEATHER   129

21 A LAWYER'S CHOICE: WHEN PASSION TURNS INTO
    OBSESSION   140

22 LUST AND OTHER DEMONS   149

23 ULURU: A TRIP TO AUSTRALIA'S RED CENTER 159

24 BECAUSE IT HAS TO FEEL RIGHT   167

25 BALI: THE LAND OF A THOUSAND TEMPLES AND A
    MILLION DISASTERS   172

26 WHEN AN INTERVIEW GOING WELL LANDS YOU THE
    WRONG JOB   181

27 MISTRESSES AND OTHER COMPLICATIONS   190

28 A ROSE IN AMSTERDAM   195

29 PARIS: LA VIE EN ROSE   202

30 WHEN FRIENDSHIP MARRIES LUST   209

31 A KNOT, SOME WORDS AND WE'RE ALL DONE 216

32 ONE QUESTION: WILL YOU PICK UP WHEN YOUR
    DREAMS ARE CALLING?   221

WHEN
DREAMS
are
CALLING

WORDS HAVE POWER, DREAMS HAVE POWER, WE HAVE POWER

1.

"ONCE UPON A TIME, there was a beautiful girl, who all day long dreamed of marrying a prince, make little princes and princesses and live happily ever after."

"Grandma, stop! This is boring!"

"Why, my child?"

"Because it's not real."

"The reality might be more boring than you expect, my dear."

"No! My reality will be the way I want it to be! My reality will be fun, exciting, and adventurous!"

And so it was. That day, I learned my first lesson: Words have power, dreams have power, we have power.

2.

My name is Dora.
Nationality: I collect, you pick.
Place of birth: Somewhere in Romania.
Date of birth: Once you know me it becomes obvious:
I was born in the year of the strutting peacock. I'm a
Rooster, although technically a Hen.
Principle place of residence: My head.
Profession: Happiness hunter.
Status: In a lifelong love-hate relationship with my
ego.
Wanted: Dead or alive and never in between.

And this is a story about change: What it brings into
our lives and what it takes out if it; a story about pain,
disappointment, frustration, loss but also about
courage, love, lust, faith and kindness; a story about
dreams and our power to make them come true.
The story of a permanent traveler.

PART ONE

THE WAKE-UP CALL

CHAPTER 1

THE WORLD OF A DREAM CHASER

If making kids is lots of fun,
When they grow up, shout, and run!

"KNOCK! KNOCK! I'M COMING! Is everyone ready for me?"

"Sure we are, sweetie!"

"Think again!"

"We'll name you Dora, Dora from adorable!"

Little did they know...

And here I was: a tiny child, covered in black hair, with two sets of eyebrows, refusing to eat alone, to sleep alone, and even to cry alone. I loved company and I made sure everyone knew that. There was no way my parents could deny me this pleasure, neither for two minutes, nor for two hours. The rules were clear and each time they tried to bend them, I was there to remind them. They were the ones who wanted me, so I made sure they had me, all over them, day and night.

For reasons that can be easily understood, the most annoying moment for them must have been when I was jumping into their bed before they did, securing my spot between them. There was nothing they could do to convince me to sleep alone. Resistance was futile. But, like they say, where there's a will there's a way.

The way was revealed to them on a beautiful summer day when my curiosity went beyond the borders of our tiny apartment. In that unfortunate day for me, but lucky for them, I went out for a walk, picked a flower for my mom, and on my way back, met a sweet little boy. Suddenly, the butterflies changed direction and from flying all over my head went straight into my stomach, tickling me without mercy. Going back home was not an option anymore and the hours passed like minutes while me and my boy were holding hands, happily chattering away. Soon it was dark. But who cared? What is more magical than watching the stars with your new lover, off in your own world, talking and dreaming with your eyes wide open? Definitely the answer was not to be found in my parents' house.

By the time I decided to go back home it was late at night. My parents were sick with fear, the police were alerted, and I was about to become a famous person, far too early in life and for all the wrong reasons. But in front of the storm, I was calm and jolly, like only a child can be.

"Do you know what time it is?" my father shouted at me, waking me up to an unwanted reality.

"It's time for love, Dad. It's time for love and kisses and moon light misses."

"Wrong! It's time for bed! Where were you?"

"Me? I had the loveliest evening. I walked and I laughed, I sang and I danced. Oh Dad, it was beautiful."

"All alone, eh? Did you think of us, your parents waiting for you at home?"

"Alone? Never alone, Dad! Grandma told me loneliness is a demon that blinds your eyes, petrifies your heart and kills your spirit. In front of loneliness, we are the poorest people that ever walk the Earth. We might have a past, but we have no future. We might have everything, but still feel like we have nothing. Grandma is always right. I call her the wise old owl. No, I was not alone, Dad I went for a walk with my boyfriend," I replied proudly.

"So, now you have a boyfriend! Oh well, if you can have a boyfriend, you can surely sleep alone." He smiled victoriously and threw me into my own bed.

"Sleep alone? But Dad, you miss the point. Once I have a boyfriend, I should not sleep alone. What boyfriends are good at other than keeping me safe while I sleep?"

"We'll talk about their usage and abusage when you'll grow older."

"Older? But I've already asked him if he wants to sleep with me when you and Mommy are not home. He said yes."

"I'm surprised he didn't say: 'Oh, yeah!'"

"So, sleeping alone is what I get back for my undivided and constant affection?" I asked caressing his hands and looking into his eyes, like a cat ready to start purring.

"Women! No matter the age, they all do it! No, this is what you get for suffocating others. From now on, I'll call you: Winnie, the seducer."

"I didn't know there is a difference between love and suffocating. When you love, you don't feel suffocated. When you don't, breathing the same air makes you feel there is not enough oxygen in the room."

"First, you disappear. Then, when you come back, you're in love. And now, you think you're an expert in loneliness, romance, and who knows what else. You're a kid."

"Smart kid, eh?"

"A smart kid. Happy now? And a pain in the arse. Now, jump into bed! God be with you. And don't forget, dreams are free!"

"And reality expensive! I know, Dad."

And so, despite all the whys, my protests, and the injustice, my father's decision remained unchanged. No more jumping into bed before they did. At night, I was on my own.

Dora's Journal Notes

- *Everyone speaks, but few make sense.*
- *Brag about how beautiful your day has been and the others will immediately feel compelled to redress the balance.*
- *The best education you can give to others is your own behavior.*

After a safe eight hours sleep, the second need of every child is to eat, or at least, this is what my parents thought. However, I had different ideas. To me, food was useful in numerous ways, except the obvious one.

Firstly, out of food, especially if you are raw vegan, you could make a facial mask. I desperately tried to convince my mom of that, but stubborn as she was, she kept cleaning up both of us, scolding me in between.

Secondly, food was useful for making my frumpy grandma exercise more around the garden.

"Catch me if you can is the name of the game, Grandma! Hurry up! You are always the loser!" I used to say, running around like a busy bee.

"You barely eat anything, but your energy is up all day long. I wish I'd know your secret. It might help with those extra kilos of mine."

And one day she did. She caught me in the act.

"What do you think you're doing?" she asked me, laughing.

"Eating?" I answered back chewing my freshly picked clover and dandelion, sprinkled on top of a freshly squashed bug.

"At least I know you won't die hungry when everyone else will," she said gently.

Lastly, I found food a good source to increase my piggy bank fortune. I knew money was important ever since I saw my grandma guarding a magical drawer, full of coins and bills. Each opening of the safe was bringing a new set of emotions: while the departure of each coin was accompanied by sights, tears, and some sort of yelling, each new arrival was applauded, praised, and accompanied by a small prayer for more.

So I went in the garden and picked whatever I found my grandma was more determined to feed me with: carrots, good for the eyes; spinach, packed with iron; parsley, the best source of vitamin C. Once safely stored, I packed them, took them to the market, and waited.

"Are you lost, child?" a nice old woman asked me.

"Do I look lost to you? I am just fine, thank you," I said, upset on her remark.

Then, another one stopped by:

"Where are your parents? Should I call the police?"

"My parents are working, the police are busy and as you can see I'm working too. Respect the workers and support the hawkers."

No one wanted to know the only thing I cared about: how much I sold my veggies for. Clearly, no one was supportive of my initiative. I was so annoyed. And my annoyance transformed into anger when my father came up to me visibly upset and embarrassed, threw away my beloved veggies, and started to lecture me about how a girl in our family should behave:

"A good girl listens to her parents, eats everything on her plate, and doesn't throw away food."

"But Dad, I did not throw it away. You did. I would have made money with it, if you didn't intervene!"

"I'm always in your way, am I?"

"You kind of are. But that's Ok, I can handle you. Mom can."

"You can, can you? Two witches: you and your mom. '
"Two fairies, Dad."
"For every woman who thinks she's a fairy, there is a man who will tell you she's not. Now, listen: there are certain things a young lady, fairy or witch, does not do; and selling veggies at the market is one."
"Lady, such a bizarre word! What kind of lady: dinner lady, tea lady, bag lady?"
"Acting silly won't help you Dora. Not now. You know very well what kind of lady I'm talking about."
"Then, I don't want to be a lady, except for first lady. Plus, I could have made some money!"
"Next time when you want to make some money use your brain, not your back."
"What about using an opportunity, Dad..."

Dora's Journal Notes

- *Try to be entrepreneur; stop listening to your family choir.*
- *When a child goes for a jog, he takes his job seriously. Keep up!*

Well-rested and well-fed, I was always ready to speak my mind and say the right things to the wrong people. The truth be told, I never figured it out when something was appropriate to say and when it was not so. The bare notion of appropriateness remained as strange to me as driving a manual car. Of course, I could have tried to understand, learn and practice both. But, I did not want to. In a world full of grey, I wanted to be either the black sheep or the white dove.

One day, when a friend of my mom's kept admiring herself in the mirror, I put a blunt stop to her dreams and I told her my honest, uncensored opinion:

"It's the ugliest dress I've ever seen. You look like a big Halloween pumpkin in it. Or like a stranded whale. Or maybe like a giant orange birthday balloon ready to burst. Or..."

"Dora, behave! Apologize immediately! And next time only speak if you have something nice to say. Otherwise, keep your opinions to yourself!" my mom said, visibly ashamed.

"But Mom, what is the purpose of having an opinion if I'm not allowed to express it? Plus, it was the truth. You taught me to always tell the truth," I went on.

"An opinion is not the truth," my mom replied bluntly.

"But out of all opinions, one has to be. It might not be the most flattering, it might not be what you'd like to hear. Nevertheless, it might be the truth. And one should learn to rise higher than their ego and appreciate honesty."

"Are you done now girl?"

"Yes, I am."

"Thank you."

"It's OK, she's right. The dress doesn't suit me," my mom's friend jumped in. "Pretending is the adults' game. Children are the best friends we can ever have. At least we know they will never lie to us. Your daughter will earn many friends..."

"And many enemies too," mom added frowning.

"Who wants to be friends with lawyers anyhow?" I said happily jumping around.

"Liars you mean, my girl."

"Yes, liars, lawyers, all the same, Mom."

Dora's Journal Notes

- *Wise is the one who knows the right time for a lie and the wrong time for the truth.*
- *If you want to see a woman again, tell her she is beautiful. No buts or ifs.*
- *Nobody remembers your mistakes better than your child, followed closely by your spouse.*

After going through the first period of my life overfed, being brutally honest, and falling in and out of my parents' bed, my first day of school finally knocked on my door.

Although most people went to school at six, my grandma, who was a teacher and the authority on the matter, solemnly declared:

"Dora will go to school at seven, so she can enjoy her childhood for as long as she can."

"Thank you, Grandma," I said softly.

Then, she continued:

"This girl, once in school, will be in it for a long time."

She didn't know how right she was.

On my first day of school, because I was shortsighted, my mom advised me to go and get a first-row seat.

I should have listened to her. Instead, I did it my way. At the end of the day, she found me sitting in the last row, as far from the scary teachers as I could, watching out the window, the autumn leaves falling down gracefully one by one and dreaming of faraway places. I wondered what they said to each other before falling down? Did they say their goodbyes? Did they weep wishing to live one more day as we do? Or were they happy to start traveling carried by the wind who knows where. Maybe both.

On the second day of school, my dad ordered me to stay away from boys and gypsies. Although they are the largest minority in the country, gypsies are perceived to bring shame to any Romanian. They have the life of a nomad, never fully accepted, never fully loved and never fully understood, but always deserving to be, same as everyone else.

I should have listened to him. Instead, I did it my way. Curious to find out what it felt like, I experienced my first kiss on the bench near school with a gypsy boy. When I came home, like a good girl, I kept my dad up to date and informed him of my latest adventure. Much has been said, but to keep it simple, I'd just say he was not happy. After the storm passed, having secrets started to sound like a good idea. In time, I learned that with parents, secrets become scolding opportunities, which later on develop either in some kind of overbearing guilt, possibly shame or even worse in some unjustified paranoia, while with the rest of the world, secrets become just weapons of mass destruction. And so, the irony is that, the most delicious ones, the ones that define us, are usually buried deep inside us or left on the death bed to some estranged nephew in an old well-guarded journal. This is when I started my journal, Dora's Journal.

Other than that, I remember the days of school fondly. My parents had a huge library where I used to spend countless happy hours with my best friends. Running my fingers down their spine, letting that powerful, unmistakable smell fill my nostrils, carried me away into a different, better world: the world of imagination.

How many tears each book has seen falling? How many laughs it heard around it? How many dreams it made come true and how many others it crashed?

I traveled with Jules Verne around the world, fell in love with the Australian outback and Ralph de Bricassart in *The Thorn Birds*, I vowed to see justice done with Edmond Dantès in *The Count of Monte Cristo*, I cried and I laughed, I paused and I marveled at the beauty of love, of friendship, of the whole world. Each day I lived another story, I traveled to another place, I followed another one's destiny.

Books had healing, magic powers. They were my spiritual retreat, my beach hideaway, my log cabin with majestic mountain views, that wonderful, exciting place where I could escape when the world was a lonely or just a dull place.

I was taking a peek into others' lives without getting caught.

I was told secrets I did not have to keep.

I was traveling back and forth in time, without getting stuck in an inconsistent causal loop.

I was falling in love without paying the price.

"One day, my name will be on one of those books, Grandma. One day, I will be a writer. If nothing else, I will have a huge library with high ceilings and big windows facing a peaceful garden with Lilac and Linden trees surrounded by marigold and poppy flowers and bushes of lavender and rose."

"When we are born, we are a book, a book with empty pages, my child. Each day, we write one more page, each day we give a new twist to our story and each turn we take sets the kind of book we are to become. Some will be romance, others will be dramas, some will be religion, others will be science, some will be action, others will be philosophy.

Your name is already on a book, my dear. The most important book you will ever write: your book. As you keep writing, just make sure that when you'll get to the end of it, you will want to read it again. Always ask yourself: what book do you want to be."

"I want to be a travel book, an inspirational, humorous travel book, Grandma."

"And you should not let anything and anybody stop you."

Dora's Journal Notes

- *Each period of our lives might be better than the next one. Hang on to what you have, be merry, and start enjoying the present.*
- *More happiness can be found living incognito than being in the spotlight.*
- *Trust your instincts. Sometimes even the advice given with the best intention in mind can be wrong.*
- *Don't think you know everything and don't rely on others to know everything.*

What soothes our hearts when we are in pain? What expresses our feelings when we are in love?

My mom thought, for every educated girl, music does. She loved piano, while I loved guitar. This time I had to listen to her and so, I started to play the piano at the local music school when I was six years old.

Everyone was a musician on our floor and all that was missing for us to become famous was a conductor. But we could never decide who would be the one, and so, we remained what we were: amateurs.

Despite this obvious fact, my neighbors were always supportive. Not my dad though. He hated it. And Mozart was the worst.

"This is not music, this is noise!"

"This is the music of my time, Dad," I replied each time playing virtuous louder and louder.

"Mozart? Sure... *Your* time, smarty pants ..."

After I left my parents' house, I didn't have a piano and I stopped practicing. Over the years, I completely forgot how to and all my efforts went down the drain. But I can still remember the examination's period when, sitting in front of a whole auditorium with my hands shaking and sweaty, I was playing three pieces of classical music by heart: Beethoven, Bach, and. ..I forgot!

"Why can't I play the composers I enjoy, Mom? I like Chopin or Rachmaninoff. They have a heart, it loves, it hates, it beats. But Bach? I hate Bach. It sounds so boring, so predictable, so baroque! You could fall asleep and still not miss much."

"In life, you play by the rules."

"Sure, *my* rules!"

Dora's Journal Notes

- *Everything that can be learned can be forgotten.*
- *Too much law, order, and care can spoil even the simplest of pleasures.*
- *Listen and learn from others' criticism. It will tell you as much about you as it will about them.*

CHAPTER 2

BUCHAREST: THE LITTLE PARIS

Take your chariot and go,
Leave behind all that you know,
But make sure before you do,
The reasons you have are valid too!

WHEN I WAS IN THE SECOND GRADE, my parents decided to leave behind the serenity of a small patriarchal city surrounded by mountains and move to the capital of Romania, Bucharest.

I am clueless on how long it took them to reach this decision, but I can safely assume it was taken in the blissful state of haste against everyone's wishes other than their own. Of course, they will never admit that. Parents know everything, they take all the decisions after careful consideration and always in the interest of the child. And dare to say any different. But, you can think differently, just not out loud. Same as with everything else in life. Until mandatory brain chips, thinking is still legally allowed.

Our arrival in Bucharest was exciting, nerve-wracking, and, for a moment or two, we all felt like we'd been thrown in at the deep end with the speed of a comet. But we were determined to hang on.

Through my eyes, the whole city looked like a huge mental institution with patients free to roam around and no doctors on duty to sedate them. Everyone was always in a hurry, parties were held in the middle of the night until the wee hours of the morning, and everywhere you looked, you could only see buildings and more buildings, trams and more trams, cars honking, bus squeaking and all the signs of a flourishing economy. I'll refrain from saying flourishing civilization. This will be a challenge to find anywhere on Earth now.

You could not walk, you were pushed around. You could not run, you were stuck. You moved in the rhythm they moved and they moved as a tortoise ready to say its last prayers.

Fight-or-flight. Survive or die. Toughen up or get crossed over. People were coming out from everywhere: from the subways, from the buildings, from the malls. There was no escape. And no time to lose. Run. But where? There was nowhere to run, or to hide, to breath or to pause, no place to die or live in peace.

All those people seem to have one thing in common and that was MSD: Mass Stress Disorder.

No one talked, but everyone yelled.

The neighbors did not know or care about each other, unless there was some major broken pipe or some rent to be paid.

And I don't deny it. Some might have thrived in that noisy, dusty chaos. Lucky them, when the world population will hit seven billion, they will survive. But not me. And to say I hated it, it would be an understatement. I vouched I will never live in big cities, be it Lima, New York, or Bucharest. I vouched to be bored with silence, nature, and stories. I vouched to have time to breath, to pause, to think, to love, to listen, to care.

But for now, I was in the mad men city, the modern European capital of Bucharest, the little Paris of the East.

When we entered the building we moved into, I felt like I'd entered an Egyptian tomb: the hallways were filled with dim light, it was quiet, and I was waiting for a mummy to touch my hand at any moment and take me away from everything which was dear to me. I was terrified.

"From now on, you'll go to school and come back from school by yourself! You'll warm up your lunch, do your homework, and wait for us to come home. You are a big, responsible girl now," my mom solemnly informed me.

"When did this growing up business happen, Mom?"
"Today."

"Wow! That was fast!"

For the following years, I could only think of how happy I was back in my small town, playing in my grandma's backyard with my friends, listening to her happy voice calling me for lunch, breathing in the clean fresh mountain air, and sharing the fish that my grandpa had caught with the entire neighborhood. Back there, the days were passing slowly, people had time to fall in love, to read, to get together, to know and help each other. The houses were beautiful and tidy, the streets were clean and everyone took pride in the natural beauty surrounding them. Back there life had the same rhythm it had for centuries. Sure there was progress, but there was also life. And it was easy to keep everything in balance.

Oh, how I missed it all. Alone in the big city, surrounded by people too busy for their own families, all I could see around were those huge buildings which, like big monsters, were crushing my universe, my sense of belonging, my peace. Here, I was just a number, a name, and an address. I was a no one.

Dora's Journal Notes

- *A big city full of opportunities that you don't want values far less than a small city full of friends and laughter.*
- *Reality is less important than our perception of it.*
- *If we juggle everything at once, we might drop the most important piece and not even notice.*

CHAPTER 3

PUPPY LOVE

When you grow up and love a boy,
Your parents might think that it's a joy.
For you it will be a tragedy in disguise,
Before you know it, you'll fall in love with all the
other guys.

IF YOU ARE NEITHER PRECOCIOUS nor slow, your first love is always happening while you are in primary school. Some lucky ones will know when it happens, live it to the fullest, and remember the person all their lives. Others will realize it happened after it ends, and with time, will barely remember who it was with.

I remember all my love affairs like they were the ones and only. I've always been hungry for a new love, for the hopes and dreams that it brings, and for how young it makes us feel no matter our age. As if I knew it would be a long list, I started to fall in love early in life.

He was blonde with blue eyes, daring, handsome, charming, and underprivileged. I was dark with green eyes, bouncy hair, beautiful, and shy. At the time, I was reading *Lady Chatterley's Lover* with a particular interest on the paragraphs where she, rich, glamorous, sophisticated, and married, was giving herself to him. a poor, uneducated servant, totally and unconditionally, crossing the social class barrier between them, bowing in front of love and defying the strict norms imposed by the society through the institution of marriage. Although their love, instead of bringing with it the security of a home was actually destroying it, she was utterly happy experiencing pure lust in the arms of the one she loved. Away from the reality brought by each ray of sun, they were living their lives fully, claiming their right to happiness. In the name of love, would they find the courage to leave it all behind and run? Being romantically inclined, I was convinced I would leave all the riches and security in the world for the sake of true love.

I was lying in bed, imagining how one night, my dear blonde and me, blue eyed boy, would passionately kiss and run away, have kids, and live happily ever after in a tiny, modest cottage far from prying eyes and unfair prejudice.

For him, I was willing to go till the end of the world and back. At that age this simply meant to play soccer with him and his friends on rainy days, all wet and covered in mud, but happy to be close to him, or to throw pebbles at his window, trying to get a last glimpse of him before going to bed. In just about each second of my life, my thoughts were with him. The poems I was writing were dedicated to him, the dresses I was buying were just for him to like me and my kisses were all kept for him. He was my inspiration, my reason to wake up and the permanent subject of all the discussions with my mom. Some might call it love, others might downgrade it to infatuation, but whatever you decide to name it, one thing was sure: I was all over him.

But one day, without any notice given to myself or to him, everything changed.

"I don't love him anymore, Mom."

"Don't worry, you never loved him, you just liked him. But how do you know that?"

"I found out today when he told me he will go to the worst high school with all the losers."

"And, what does this have to do with love?"

"Everything. I could forgive him for being a terrible kisser and a forgetful boyfriend, for his less than desirable origins, for his lack of manners, and for whatever other shortcomings, but I could never ever forgive his lack of ambition."

"So, no tears, no pain, no sleepless nights and no remorse."

"None of it. It's plain and simple. I'm not in love anymore."

"The mind conquered the heart. I just hope all your breakups will go as smooth as this one."

"I'll make sure to leave them first," I replied, giving her a wink.

Dora's Journal Notes

- *You can always exercise just by running after guys.*
- *Love should stand first the test of the brain, then the test of heart, and only then it might pass the test of time.*
- *In books, love is overly romanticized. In reality, love is just complex. Enjoy both.*
- *People live in reality, but thrive on illusions.*

When I was done dreaming about all the handsome guys, dark or blonde, with green or blue eyes, shy or daring, I prayed for a real man: one with ordinary looks but an extraordinary brain, with ordinary eyes, but an extraordinary heart. However, I forgot to mention one little tiny thing: one ordinary in public, but extraordinary in bed. And this slip of the mind proved to be fatal.

I met him when I was sixteen. He was an average-looking guy, smart, and with a warm heart. He loved me to bits. To show it to me, he bought me donuts, roses, took me to opera, listened to all my fears, and chased away my demons. There was nothing he refused me.

After five years of a relationship, we finally decided it was time. We jumped naked into bed, full of hopes and longtime plans. Despite him having all the desires more or less obvious, I had no other desire except for falling asleep. Kissing him felt like a duty, touching him seemed a waste of time, and letting him to do all these to me was almost unbearable.

"The clothes are off, I got on top of you, now what? How long until it starts to feel good?" he joked.

"Not sure, but I have a headache already," I answered, joining the "happily involved" women club, the ones whose answer is always a headache.

Our sexuality, instead of being a dream taking us to highs of deep pleasures, was bringing us to lows of deep sadness. Far from an empowering experience, it was humiliating and stressful. We were great friends, but impossible lovers.

When all this physical intimacy became a burden, causing grief and threatening to break my otherwise perfect relationship, not knowing what to do, I mustered all my courage and asked my mom about it:

"Mom, why do I always get a headache when he wants to touch me? Is there anything wrong with me?"

"In life, my dear, there are two kinds of men: one who give you a headache and other who make all the headaches go away. Headaches are a good sign to know which one you'll choose."

"What do you mean? Should I leave him because he's a bust in bed? Will I ever find another sweet soul to be there when no one else is, to love my mistakes just because they are mine, and on top of that, be a skilled perfect lover?"

"Who knows? But should you let fears to rule your world?"

"I wish there would be a way to stop thinking about it, to stop wanting to feel how it is to make passionate love. He's such a wonderful guy."

"Just remember, no amount of food will ever replace a drop of water."

And right she was. Like a flame, my strong sexual desires were burning everything in their way waiting for that moment when weak, tired, or maybe just wise, I would stop fighting them.

While our friendship got stronger every year, our romance never blossomed.

Dora's Journal Notes

- *Only by being faithful to love, not to your lover, you will find happiness.*
- *Sexuality is a gift that should never be denied.*

CHAPTER 4

A CAREER: BETWEEN PASSION AND CHORE

Picking a career, one might say,
Can be tricky all the way.
But if others pick for you,
Tell them straight to do it too!

ON YOUR FIRST BIRTHDAY in Romania, there is a custom where the elder ones put different objects on a table and let you grab any three of them. Then, depending on your choice, they make suppositions on what you'll become in life. I chose books, money, and books again. My parents' verdict was simple: I was to be either a lawyer or a doctor. No more and no less. The perfect careers, which marry books and money.

"Think about the financial security, the respect that being a doctor or a lawyer commands, and the position in the society it offers! Your life will be easy and happy," my parents declared when I had to choose what university I would attend.

"I don't know about that. It doesn't feel right."

"And what do you think it will?"

"I want to be a writer, a gardener, or even a chef and travel the world. Nothing would make me happier than that. I want to spend my days with my hands in the soil, sing along with the wind and the birds, wish for rain and pray for sun, write about the beauty and mystery of life. If I could do all that, I think I'll be happy and proud."

"Writers die poor, you travel after you already have enough money to live forever after, you plant veggies in your retirement, and you won't need to cook once you have the money to go to a restaurant. Take that nonsense out of your mind. You'll do as you're told. One day you'll thank us for it," my dad proclaimed.

"Then, if I must, I'll be a lawyer!" I replied furiously.

"Why did you pick law?" my dad asked, curiously.

"Because of the prestige, the charisma that seems to go with it, the supposed smartness that accompanies each and every lawyer on their way to the court. Because this is what *you* want!"

"Why not a doctor?" my mom jumped in, hoping I would step into her shoes.

"Doctors neither let you live free nor die in peace. They come up with a long list of must dos and then, you die doing them while others live ignoring them. They invent a pill for every ache and pain you suffer from or you imagine suffering from. They blame it on stress and forget all the rest. I'll be better off being a bastard egotistic lawyer than a know-it-all doctor."

"No offense taken," my mom replied, taken aback by my sudden outburst.

"Why should you? I am doing what you want, am I not? Now, all of you just leave me alone!" I said rushing out and slamming the door behind me.

Alone in my room, I was crying. I knew my parents had a hard time understanding and accepting my way of being. But what if they were right? What if being a lawyer or a doctor was a safe option? It's the "ifs" that are killing us. Always the "ifs."

While my parents were pushing me towards law, the entire universe was trying to keep me away from it. The first sign came when, despite being the best in my class, I failed the admission exam and I was not accepted into the best law school in the country. It was a miracle, but it was perceived as a disaster that would bring shame upon the family for generations and generations. No one could let this happen, and definitely not my parents. I was sent to a private law school where I continued to be an exceptional student, which confirmed everyone's beliefs that I would be a brilliant lawyer, one that would make everyone proud. With time, my failure became a thing of the past and life followed its normal, easy course.

However, after four years of university, when I was a step away from becoming a lawyer, instead of being excited, I was scared and instead of feeling liberated, I felt lost.

Although I couldn't explain why, to me, practicing law felt terribly wrong.

"I don't think I'm cut for being a lawyer, Mom!"

"You're just a bit scared. It's perfectly normal. Once out of school, you'll start a new phase in your life. Don't worry! You'll be an excellent lawyer, perhaps even a famous judge."

"But what if I won't?"

"Stop this nonsense! Everyone in our family is a lawyer, a doctor or an engineer! Why do you think you're any different?"

"You make it sound like being different is something bad."

"In this case, it is! You'll be a great lawyer. I don't want to hear about it any longer."

When she said that, I felt like a puppet. There was nothing I wanted more than to break free. But, I was clueless on how I could make this happen.

Over the time, my panic attacks and anxiety took over. Frightened and confused, once again all I wanted was to be a writer, a gardener, or even a chef and travel the world.

Dora's Journal Notes

- *Never be swayed by others' expectations.*
- *Don't let pride and fear stand between you and your dreams.*
- *Choose the content over the label. Choose the person over the title. Choose the truth over the appearances.*
- *Believing you know what is best for your kids is like believing the future will be identical to the past.*
- *Feelings are not thoughts to be explained. Go with them and the explanation will follow.*
- *Let others' experiences be your compass, but always choose to be the one at the helm.*
- *Being good at something does not mean you cannot be happier doing something else. You owe it to yourself to find what that is.*
- *Advice that is imposed on others becomes a command.*
- *Don't ask your children to be something they are not. Instead, teach them how to make the most of who they are.*

CHAPTER 5

DEPRESSION: AN OPPORTUNITY OR A CURSE

When the clouds of a storm are high above
And we feel lost with no chance to rise off the ground,
We might pay a dear price and talk to him
Our psychiatrist, doctor, who's happy and slim.
He might give us a pill to throw us into sleep,
But when awake we might feel worse than a dead
sheep.
That's why you should take my advice and do as I say
Ignore depression and it will soon fly away!

WHEN I DIDN'T WANT TO READ any book or go outside, when I just wanted to sleep all day and everything seemed to trigger tears, pain, and a sense of loss, when food had no flavor and each morning I could feel a cold sweat down my spine, I knew I was depressed.

There are many ways in which you can go about a depression.

Usually, you start by a fairly comprehensive analysis of its roots.

So, what was it? Was I too sensitive, reading too much poetry, too much Freud, too much psychology? Hardly, as I was always excited and happy with all of these activities.

Were my sex hormones going cuckoo? Did I need some *therapeutic sex sessions*? If that was so, everyone will want to be depressed and cured, then cured and depressed and so on.

Was it genetic? This one is always hard to say, for the simple reason that some people hide depression so well, that from the outside they look better than anyone else around. But, as far as I knew, from my ten years old sister to my ninety-five years great grandpa, everyone was in amazingly good health.

Could I have blamed it on my parents, on their rules and high expectations that were shutting the gates to my dreams like the guardian shutting the door of the prison cell, giving the one inside no option than to wait and hope? Definitely too much Freud.

But, like with airplane crashes, it's never only one factor; it's always a combination. So, go figure.

After the causes are covered and uncovered, you move on to remedies, the only thing that truly matters.

Let's take them one by one: reflexology. I worked the toes, the top of my feet, the arch of the feet, the inside and outside of them, day and night, hard, then harder, then even harder, following a simple principle: more pain outside, less pain inside. But all of my work was to no avail. At the end of each session, I had happy feet, but nothing else changed.

Then, I went into astrological aromatherapy, which tells which essential oil suits you according to your sun sign. Sensuous, mysterious, erotic, uplifting, excellent for nervous tension, sandalwood was ideal for me, a true born Aquarius. Maybe the oil was not good, maybe I was not the run-of-the-mill Aquarius, whatever it was, it failed. At least I got to smell nice each day.

Homeopathy was another interesting option. For mild depression, anxiety and all those wonderful ailments, aconitum, the queen and the king of poisons, was the answer. But only in books. In reality, I was immune to it.

During all these experiments and thinking and brooding, I've learned a few things. For example, depression is a controlling, selfish, manipulating beast, craving attention. And whenever my attention was waning, her grip on me was becoming weaker too. Like any predator, depression was not praying on the strongest, but on the weakest.

Then, depression let me get plenty of rest. In fact, that's all I wanted to do and all I did: rest. I rested my body and troubled my mind.

I was also in the position to fully argue that talk is not cheap. Quite the contrary, talk can be terribly expensive And the first visit to the psychiatrist proved the point. In fact, it did it so well, that I was forced to consider not going back for the second session.

And one last important bit: suddenly I had some peace and quiet. People treated me like I'd had some kind of contagious disease and gave me plenty of space.

But, besides those small perks, living with depression, or more accurately simply existing, was not fun.

I was scared I'd never have a husband, a job, a family and no one would ever want me.

I was terrified something was terribly wrong with me and that I was different for all the wrong reasons.

Many times I wondered why it had to happen to me, why God, out of all people, chose to punish me. Was it a test? If it was, I was failing it completely. Was it some kind of sign? If it was, I was not getting it. Maybe I had to have patience, to wait. But since when waiting gets us anywhere?

But, I enjoyed lamenting about it. It was the only thing left for me to do. And I did it, day after day until my mom, got tired of it:

"So many others would like to be in your shoes, to be born to such a family. You should feel blessed for all you have, for being beautiful and intelligent and for having the opportunity to become a lawyer. You have no reason to feel this way. You're acting like a spoiled child."

"Reasons and feelings, why they always have to go together? You talk as if I choose to feel this way. But I don't. If I knew what to do to feel better, I would."

Their know-it-all attitude frustrated me. I wanted their compassion, not judgment. I wanted to feel their love, not the burden of guilt for making them feel disillusioned with me.

Each day I was hoping to find some miraculous cure which would make everyone happy again.

And one day, I did:

"What if my depression is not a curse, but my opportunity to change my life radically? An opportunity to do something that will excite my tired mind, will free my enchained spirit, and will give me again the choices I had missed," I asked myself looking in the mirror.

A new chance, A chance to cut the apron strings, my inner voice answered.

"Yes, a chance to master my own destiny and build a new life, completely different from what I had and what is planned for me to have. A life forged by me, with my own failures and my own achievements, a life in which I'd fight for my own dreams. A life worth living. My own adventure."

And how exactly do you propose to do that?

"There are moments in life when making small changes it's not enough. You cannot build a brand new house on the same shifting soil."

You need to be a tabula rasa again.

"Or close to it. I need to be far away from my parents' pressure, away from any preconceived ideas about how should I be or what should I do. I could go to Canada. When I visited my mom's cousin in Montreal, I loved it there."

You could give it a try. Plus, she might be able to help you in times of need.

"Worse come to worse, I could always come back."

Worse will become even worse if you'll come back.

"Canada will be my adventure. 'A ship is safe in harbor, but that's not what ships are built for.' I believe it was William Shedd who said that."

So, go with the wind. But, you have no plan. You barely speak any English and even if you would, your law degree is not recognized. You've never done anything in your life, except of reading books. You don't even know how to make two fried eggs.

"I'll just have to play it by ear. The best plan is nothing more than confidence that everything will work out for the best, is it? It must be a way. And I will find it."

Dora's Journal Notes

- *Depression is not a choice, but an unwanted and predictable outcome of a series of unhappy choices.*
- *Don't try to explain to others how depression feels like; try to learn from them what is to see beyond it.*
- *Accept you are a work in progress, that there are things which you cannot change, others which take time to change and some which will be a shame to change.*
- *If you are living a dream and you are still depressed, check if you are not living someone else's dream.*
- *Don't be afraid of feeling sad; it might be just the push you need for making another attempt at happiness.*
- *Life is simple, living it is complicated.*

CHAPTER 6

FAMILY IS FOREVER: HAZARD OR BLESSING

Family, we all might think
Is a "bloody" kind of thing,
I believe it's more about
Love and support
Be it sunny or cloud'.

WHILE SOME PEOPLE ARE FOLLOWERS, love routine, and thrive on order, others are leaders, love adventure, and thrive in chaos. Irrespective on how each of us is, one thing is certain: no progress would be possible and the world would be a boring place if we were all identical.

Same as we need dark to rest and light to live, same as events are generated in noise and thought of in quiet, each of us has his own role in the world, his own mission to fulfill. For some, it will be easier to recognize it; others might search for it their entire life, but nobody should ever doubt that they are needed somewhere and worth loving by someone.

There is no other place like home, where we feel more the need of being accepted for what we are. All our life, we flourish on our family's support and approval and we wilt on its disdain and criticism.

At home, we should be loved the way we are. Our family should be our refuge, our place to rest, to gather strength and courage, to feel joy and confidence, our sanctuary. In a family, it should never matter how different we are from each other. Family should be about unity, not individuality, about tolerance, not compatibility.

I was an explorer, of people, of places and of myself. I was allergic to any limitations on my freedom, fond of everything that was new or just a bit different, willing to take risks, unpredictable, oblivious to the society's whims of fashion, and always ready to look on the bright side of things. Monotony tired me, adventure excited me and following others crippled me. My only constant was change.

My parents loved rules, making plans and sticking to them. They were prone to predict the worst, strived on routine and security, and had fixed ideas about what makes one smart, successful, and happy.

Despite loving me to bits, they could never accept me the way I was and tried to mould me into someone else. Their support was dependent on their consent and their warmth and kindness were present as long as obediently, I was playing the role that was given to me. My decisions were never respected, but argued; my wishes were never accepted, but questioned.

Over the years, I felt trapped between my desire to please them and the need of being myself. I wanted to be free to choose my own way of life without being afraid of upsetting them. I knew one day I would break free. I just never knew when or how.

Now, that it was finally happening, I felt relieved, like a huge burden was about to be taken off my shoulders. And if leaving behind my country and my dear ones was the price I had to pay for it, then so be it. Freedom was all I wanted and I was not willing to haggle for it.

However, for them, my departure was a shock. It came all of a sudden, gave them no warning and no chance to prepare. They were confused and hurt, betrayed and disappointed. In their eyes, my life was perfect. After all, I was surrounded with love. What more could I have wanted? What more was it out there that they could not provide me with? So, being a spoiled brat, was their only explanation for my depression and for my radical departure.

Maybe they were right, maybe I was a spoiled brat, who had it all, and as a change, wanted to see how it is to have nothing. Maybe, taking off all alone in the big world out there was a crazy idea. Maybe, I should have taken a good look around at what I had before jumping on a new adventure and hurting everyone who was dear to me.

Or maybe not. Maybe their pain was self-inflicting pain. A temporary burst vanishing away as soon as they would realize that what could be interpreted as a crazy act of disobedience was in fact an act of courage and faith, an act of love, the ultimate love, the love for freedom. Something I had to do if I wanted to find happiness. It was not their fault, same as it wasn't mine. It was no one's fault. They had their own identity. I still had to find mine. Same as there's so much a young tree can grow in the shadow of the old one, there is so much a youngster can learn and experience living in the shadow of his parents.

The truth is that no one could know for sure what was better for me. And maybe, just maybe, they should've left it at that. And above everything else, just love me.

Dora's Journal Notes

- *In life, no matter what we are doing, there will always be people who like us and others who don't. Be yourself and choose to be liked by the ones alike.*
- *When you stop working so hard to fulfill others' dreams, you will have the energy to search for your own.*
- *Being a nobody has its advantages: you can be yourself.*
- *There is no absolute freedom. But when we are the ones choosing our confinements, then we feel free.*

CHAPTER 7

LEAVING THE LAND OF DRACULA

Home, sweet home, where have you been?
I looked for you in lands far in between,
The smell of grass, the song I sang,
The games I played, the friends I rang,
You are still there waiting for me,
The same old place you used to be.

NO MATTER WHERE YOU LIVE, who you marry, or how much time has passed, you will always bear the imprint of traditions, customs or just day to day habits of your native land. You will see the world and perceive the ones around you through them, because no matter right or wrong, funny or annoying, weird of just common, they will always be a part of who you are.

A few weeks before I left Romania, I could not stop thinking about what I would miss the most from the land I was born in. What memories would I recount sitting by the fire with my lover, three of his kids, two of my own, and eight of ours?

My first thought was at Christmas.

Christmas in Romania is a time to be with your whole family, to cherish your loved ones, to prepare your list for Santa, then to read the lists of all the others trying not to lose too much sleep over it.

People go to church and pray for the next year to do a better job than the current one, as any "next one" does, at least for a while...

It's not so much of a happy time as of a busy time. Everybody becomes suddenly obsessed with cleaning their apartments thoroughly, over and over again, day and night. The windows have to be immaculate so you can spy on the neighbors, the corner behind the library free of dust to look neat and tidy and each and every ornament must be cleaned and then placed back in the exact same spot. The markets are packed with fur trees, cut more unlawfully than lawfully and carrying them all around trams and buses is a pain if not necessarily for you, then for all the rest of the passengers. The men are busy with the grocery shopping, running from one store to the other, facing interminable queues, and fighting over the best piece of meat in the butchery stores just so they can come home and find their wives still not quite happy with what they have got. The Romanian women are picky, and how can they not be, when their dishes are their pride?

The most famous dish found in all the kitchens around Romania is *sarmale*, followed closely by *cozonac*. *Sarmale* are pickled cabbage leaves stuffed with a mixture of pork, rice, pepper, and other spices. If you never tried them, it might be a good time for you to reconsider. They are delicious!

The popular *cozonac* is a cake filled with walnuts, cacao, and raisins. It helps with putting on weight each time without exception and only the smell of it can turn you into a hungry impatient beast!

The holidays are all about getting stuffed: firstly, at your house and then, at everyone else's. You don't eat to live, you live to keep eating. It is considered an insult to stop before the ambulance comes.

Where there is food, there must be music. The carol singers dressed in folk costumes go from one house to another, singing till morning, and people compensate them with cakes, apples, nuts, and, best of all, money. Each family opens its door, time and time again, to lots of groups of singers, some more talented than others, but all bringing with them the spirit of Christmas.

Each party lasts until all the wine is over, usually at dawn. People dance and sing like demons walking on hot coal and no one goes to bed before the roosters wake up.

The most popular present of all time, for kids and adults, moms and dads, friends and girlfriends, is pajamas. It does not matter if you do not need one, or you just do not want one, or you never slept in one. Pajamas are always on top of the list of presents.

Christmas or no Christmas, Romanians are a passionate nation. The problem is that they are passionate about everything without distinction: passionate about what their neighbors are doing, about soccer, politics, fashion, and churches.

Soccer turns friends into foes and if you ever want to attend a big game you must be prepared to come back home with more than your ego bruised. Politics is a big nebulous and the ministers come and go before even realizing they were nominated.

Fashion is at its best and Romanian women, wherever they go, from the market to the ball on New Year, will always look carefully dressed. Stunning too. Like a cheeky advertising campaign pointed out: "Half of Romanian women look like Kate. The other half, like her sister." And this says it all. No blondes I'm afraid!

Besides being gorgeous chefs, Romanian women are pious as well. Each Sunday they attend one of the thousands of churches found on every corner, some old since the seventh century, others the newest addition on the block, to wash away their sins, pray for some more to come, or just listen to others' adventures.

All this buzzing and running around keeps Romanians young. As a proof, Radu Beligan, a ninety-five years old Romanian actor, has entered the Guinness book of World Records for being the oldest actor on stage. But, don't worry, even if you're not an actor, you can still make it! Just make sure you get the right Romanian genes!

But sooner or later, even a Romanian is put to rest. Tucked away in a tiny village of Maramures county, the Merry Cemetery *(Cimitirul Vesel)* reminds every visitor that even there, in the afterlife kingdom, be it heaven or hell, Romanians insist on being the cheerleaders. Its colorful high wooden crosses are painted with scenes of the deceased's life and have written all over witty poems depicting the life of the person buried there. At Merry Cemetery, death does not stop one from laughing.

One of the most famous and funniest epitaphs is the one addressed to a mother-in-law:

> *Underneath this heavy cross*
> *Lies my poor mother in-law*
> *Three more days should she have lived*
> *I would lie, and she would read.*
> *You, who here are passing by*
> *Not to wake her up please try*
> *Cause' if she will again rise*
> *She'll do nothing but despise*
> *But I will surely behave*
> *So she'll not return from grave.*

The optimistic spirit of the people is also present in typical superstitions, such as if you cry at your wedding or if it's been pouring all day, then you'll be happy in your marriage. I was never told what would happen if, as some might wish, it's sunny. I guess, you could always compensate for the weather with some heavy crying.

In Romania, old traditions such as *Martisor*, are still alive. Martisor celebrates the beginning of spring and before, everyone used to offer a red and white string from which a small decoration is tied. Rumor has it the one wearing it will prosper in the coming year. Nowadays, only the men offer it to the women they fancy. No wonder the country is not prospering anymore.

If the Western world has Valentine's, Romanians have Valentine and *Dragobete*. Celebrated on the twenty-fourth of February, it's a traditional ancient holiday, when boys and girls pick spring flowers, kiss and sing about the beauty of love. It's been said that, while dancing, the one who steps over the partner's foot, will take the lead in the relationship. And, as any Romanian man is less of a dancer, this superstition will easily explain why, in most Romanian families, the women have the last say.

For all that it is and for all that it's not, but most of all for what it meant to me, I knew I will miss Romania, the land of Decebal and Dracula, Brancusi and Nadia Comaneci, Emil Palade and Gheorghe Zamfir. The land of my soul.

Dora's Journal Notes

- Memories are subjective perceptions of an objective reality.

PART TWO

CANADA, LEARNING THE ART OF LIVING

"The great themes of Canadian history are as follows: keeping the Americans out, keeping the French in, and trying to get the Natives to somehow disappear."

Will Ferguson

CHAPTER 8

THERE IS NO OTHER TRIP LIKE THE ONE WE EMBARK ON FINDING OURSELVES

*A new beginning brings with it
More hope, more luck, more love within.
It might be bumpy at the start,
But once in it, just play your part.
Believe in it, believe in you,
Hang on in there and stay true!*

SOME PEOPLE LOOK AT IMMIGRATION as a simple change of countries: you land, get a job, raise a few kids and life goes on much happier than before.

But the truth is, immigration is more than that, it's building everything from scratch. It takes not only luck, but also courage, not only courage, but also lots of work, not only work but also faith. It takes everything. But it also gives back confidence, strength and the ultimate power: the power of knowing who you are. In my eyes, all immigrants are winners.

I left Romania soon after Easter with two suitcases, one thousand dollars in my pocket, and millions of hopes. I was twenty-three years old.

During the flight to Toronto, the hours passed slowly and there was not a single minute in which I did not doubt the sanity or the necessity of the decision.

I was not happy, but excited, not afraid, but curious, not rational, but enthusiastic. I was finally the master of my own fate. This was all that mattered.

I've never been to Toronto and I was imagining it as a city full of skyscrapers, squirrels, and immigrants of all nationalities. I could just see myself figuring out one by one everything that we take for granted when we live our lives in the same place. It was a bit like one of those puzzle games, both challenging and exciting.

I was scared, but so was I each time I had to fly. But this never stopped me from traveling. Why should it? There is no greater fear than the fear of change and there is no greater joy than overcoming it. Thinking of that, slowly, I felt some sort of detachment taking over me and a deep sense of peace soon followed. I knew one way or another, I would be fine.

"Welcome to Canada," the immigration officer said to me.

"Thank you. I'm happy to be here."

And then, politely smiling at me, he put the stamp in my passport and wished me good luck.

"Thanks," I replied while thinking to myself that I'll need plenty of it.

With my hands still shaking holding the passport. I went through the final gates.

I had done it. I was on my own, away from home, looking for a new home!

The family I was supposed to stay with and baby-sit their children for picked me up from the airport.

"We have two news, a good one and a bad one," the guy said to me once we arrived home. "Which one would you like to hear first?"

A bit surprised and still dizzy from the flight, I answered:

"I think the good one will be nice to start off with."

"You can stay with us for as long as you need."

"I thought this is a given, not quite news."

"It is and it's not. In a nutshell, we brought a baby sitter from the Philippines, my wife's arrangement, and we don't need you anymore."

"That's fine, I think, I hope. I'll look for some other job," I replied trying to keep my wits together.

"This being said, the house is full and we don't have a room for you. So, I'm afraid you'll have to sleep in the garage. We'll throw a mattress somewhere there and we'll try to park the cars outside for the time being. If you pay us a few hundred dollars per month it will all work out. You don't have to rush to let me know your decision."

"But, I do have to rush," I said looking inside the garage, trying to picture myself sleeping there.

I could not process the information, as if my brain short-circuited. I could not breathe anymore and I couldn't tell if my heart stopped beating right that second when he uttered those damn words or a few moments after. While my mind was looking for a way out, my body needed something to lean on. I closed my eyes hoping that next time when they will see the light, the whole picture will change. But it didn't. I was still standing there, in that long hallway, with my two suitcases. And they were still rambling nonsense. I wanted to cry, but the tears were nowhere to be found. Nothing and nobody could wash away my pain. I had nowhere else to go and no one to talk to. I was exhausted and all I wanted was a decent meal and a bed, just as I had planned. Was that too much to ask for?

"Think, think, think," I said to myself.

Think of what? the committee in my head asked unanimously.

"Yes, you're right, not much to think of. I'd better pray. Pray for a couch."

I went for a walk around the neighborhood, trying to calm down.

"You're a lawyer. Practice your lawyering skills. Turn black into white."

Sorry, I'm a Prosecutor. I only know how to turn white into black.

"You're a Rooster. Time to dig deep."

I'm a Hen. Time to find a rooster, lay eggs and care for baby chicks. I should go back to Romania.

"Go back? That fast? Give up that easily? You're not a Hen, you're a chicken!"

Better than sleep in a garage.

"I don't remember you being too happy sleeping in a comfy bed either."

But even God has limited patience for whiners. Fed up, He answered my prayers in His own unique style: I asked for a couch, God delivered a man.

Some could argue the offer was way better than a couch. Looking back now, I could not agree more. He was not the ordinary kind of man, but the most caring, generous, and compassionate Canadian I've ever met.

"Hi. I'm Robert. You look a bit lost. Can I help you?"

"No, thank you. I'm fine."

"You don't look fine to me. But, that's ok. Just take this," he said handing me his business card.

"Thank you."

"Good talkin' to ya. Take care, eh," he said walking away.

After a while, exhausted from the physical effort, the lack of sleep, or the millions of thoughts going through my mind, I went back to the house and fell asleep right away on the old mattress waiting for me in the garage

Next morning, when I opened my eyes, I couldn't remember much.

"Where am I? Am I dreaming? Or have I died?"

Fortunately or less fortunately, you are alive.

"Thank God, heaven cannot be that bad!"

I looked around me confused and one by one it all came back to me, the landing, the discussion, the house, the stranger met down the street.

Thinking of him made me warm inside. He looked like a good-hearted person. He had a pleasant smile and seemed concerned of my well-being.

"He's a guy! Sure he must seem like that if he wants you!"

Want me? Why would anyone want me now? I'm not an asset, I'm a liability.

"You're both. All of us are both our entire life, one way or the other. But should we be with someone who thinks like an accountant? Maybe he genuinely liked you."

Maybe he did, maybe he did not! Who cares about all this now! I'm not dating him! I need him! He's my only hope. He cannot be worse than those people!

And so, I called him, gave him the address, and showed him my place in the garage.

There are some moments in life when the right words can make all the difference, and there are others when there are no right words, just facts, plain and simple facts. This was one of the latter ones.

After Robert asked my so-called hosts for my money back, we started to look for a place to rent on my own.

With no previous references and not too much money, finding something was if not impossible, surely a bit of a challenge. After a bit of driving around, from nice neighborhoods to less and less nicer ones, we found a shabby building with a shabby sign in a poor neighborhood: "Cheap rooms for rent. No references required." And this sight which once upon a time would have never met my eyes, now it filled my heart with joy.

After hard negotiations with an old Greek lady speaking neither Romanian nor English, I ended up renting a tiny bachelor apartment, disgusting, unfurnished, at the basement. However, it was all mine and for now it was much better than a garage.

And this was how my Canadian adventure started.

We are never alone. Even when we want to be left alone or when we cry in despair thinking that we are all alone, even then, we are not alone. Just blind. I made no exception. After my first night in my new "glamorous" apartment, during the wee hours of the morning, I met my new comrades. They were a healthy bunch of happy cockroaches running around, eager to multiply and always there to keep me company.

Such an offer! Who could refuse it? I could! And I did!

From a peaceful woman, I transformed into a vengeful serial killer, declared war, and focused all my energy and knowledge on winning. Probably they would never know what they had done wrong. But, I knew: they sneaked in, in large numbers, totally uninvited. And, after a few weeks of playing dirty tricks on them with different kind of poisons, I became the sole happy tenant, proving once more that the power stands in the brain, not in the numbers.

Sleeping straight on the floor, although it might have been good for my back, was never one of my favorite things. With no money to afford a bed, I ended up buying an inflatable small mattress.

From the comfort of a very nice house it was quite a change, and although it was way better than being homeless, it was not too far ahead.

So, I figured some fresh paint on the walls would make me feel a little bit more cheerful. As during the day I was too preoccupied on running around looking for jobs, I painted my burrow at nighttime. Afraid someone might break in, like I was on a secret suicide mission, I kept all the windows closed. As expected, the strong smell of the paint made me faint and for the next few days I was high, for a completely different set of reasons than one would wish to be.

I don't remember ever having as many discussions with myself as back then. It was almost like two people were residing inside my head: one was always upset, scared, frustrated and wanted to go back to Romania; the other was always trying to be the cheerleader, fiercely determined not to give up. It was hard to say which one of them was more convincing. They seemed to take turns and each day when I woke up I could never tell who will be the winner of the day:

"So, tell me, was it smart to leave my legal profession, my nice house, my friends and my own country?"

Obviously not. But hold on, things will improve. All in good time.

"Sure they will. It's not that hard to get better than this. How much better, this is a totally different question. It is bad. That's the truth."

Just make sure that what you call truth is not a produce of your mind, but of reality as is. A happy life is not necessarily a secure one, but an authentic one. This is what you wanted, isn't it? Now, don't be picky and impatient.

"Picky? You call this picky?"

If not picky, then surely prickly.

"I know the drill. You want me to be grateful for everything I have, every day I live. No questions asked. I am sorry to disappoint you, but I am not."

I want you to keep trying; to believe in yourself, in your destiny, to believe that everything will be fine. Because what you believe in, this is what will happen.

"What does not kill you makes you stronger."

And if it kills you, you are no longer.

"That's always a possibility."

As much as all this bickering back and forth was OK in Romanian, outside my head everyone spoke English or something that resembled to it. More and more, it became quite obvious to me that if I want to find a decent job, I'd better do the same.

Together with my Canadian savior and two huge dictionaries, I started to learn proper English. It was a long, frustrating process, which was taking place all the time: while eating, cooking, taking a shower, crying or looking for jobs. Soon, my body was entirely covered by self-made temporary tattoos, depicting not some forgotten lover or dead pet, but just plain English words. Not being able to say what I wanted, the way I wanted was incredibly frustrating and made me think for a second of those unfortunate enough to be born without a voice.

"Maybe it's time for me to learn the sign language," one day I said to Robert.

"Sorry, sweetie, but even the sign language is not universal. I'm afraid you're stuck with English. And with this pineapple that you'll have to eat today if you don't want to become a ghost. Later on, we could go and feed the angry geese or just listen to Michael Buble."

"I don't want any *pee-nap-uhl* and any *jeez*. And I hate that Michael *Buhb-uhl*."

"Sure, you don't, sweetie. You want *gees* and *pahy-nap-uhl*, and maybe some Michael *Boo-ble*," he corrected me gently.

"Damn it! I'm so tired..."

"You're freakin'cute! Don't worry! You'll get it!"

Day by day, the whole process was becoming easier. He was slowly learning a bit of Romanian and I was making huge progress with English.

On my birthday, Robert, with the help of master Google, wrote me a card in broken Romanian:

"*La multi ani! Sa fii fericita si iubita! Te ador!*" Meaning: "Happy Birthday! Be happy and loved! I adore you!"

When I read it, I burst into tears. His devotion to me, to my dream, to my well-being was more than anyone could ask. He must have been an angel sent by God. And so, each day I expected he would just disappear, same as he came, out of nowhere.

"Thank you," I said giving him a strong kiss on the cheek.

"You're welcome. But if you keep crying, next time I'll have to write it in English. And it would not be even half as fun as writing this one was."

"But it will be easier!"

"Pfff ! If it's easy and no fun, there's no deal, you should run."

Despite Robert's support, my first few months were miserable. I felt terribly lonely, depressed with not getting a job and very tired. My mind was tormented by questions and doubts. Nothing could have prepared me for such a different life than the one I was used to or the one I was hoping to find.

But no day was passing without promising myself that one day, I would feel at home in Canada. One day I would be a lawyer again, meaning in my mind simply that one day I will be someone again, at least more than a lost child with nothing but dreams. And this kept me going.

Dora's Journal Notes

- *There is no other trip like the one you embark on finding yourself.*
- *Adapting and belonging are two different things. Try to adapt less and belong more.*
- *Where luck fails, resilience succeeds.*
- *If people will want to help you, they will do it without too much talking and if they don't, a million of reasons will not be enough.*
- *Only when compassion translates into action, you know it is genuine.*
- *Learn from disappointment, but don't let disappointment rule you.*

CHAPTER 9

BEFORE JOBS, THERE ARE CHOICES

*Finding jobs is never dull
And most definitely not fun!
Stand your ground or simply wait,
Hope, believe, just hang on, mate!*

SOMETIMES WHAT WE LOOK FOR in faraway places, we might find close to us.

And so, after looking for jobs in newspapers without much luck, a neighbor offered me my first job in Canada.

Together with him, I installed bathtubs. The pay for my one and only day of work: a pair of cheap running shoes and a meal.

Now let me tell you that, although for a trained lawyer it was not quite exciting, it was definitely challenging. Plus no one in my family had ever installed bathtubs. For the first time, I got to be the first. Wasn't that something? I was laughing to myself imaging my poor mom's conversation with her fellow doctor friends:

"So, what is your daughter doing in Canada? Is she doing her master in law?"

"No, she's installing bathtubs."

"Wow! That's interesting..."

Did you ever wonder how come such a promising word as "interesting" is, can be used by people to mask disdain and shock? I know I did.

Leaving my mom aside, I'm not sure how my neighbor selected *me* for the job. Was it my brain or my looks to be blamed for it?

But when such "luck" strikes, you don't ask questions; you turn around.

Dora's Journal Notes

- *Not each challenge is worth taking.*
- *If I admire the ones who dare to dream, I bow before the ones who never give up on their dreams.*

My next job offer came from a woman, immigrant as well. I was sure she'd understand what being a young woman, all alone in a new country means,

After she scanned me from top to bottom, she delivered the verdict:

"You'll make a great stripper. Great money in it too."

"Are you flattering me?"

"Does it sound like a flatter to you?"

"No, not really."

"You're lucky. I know just the right person for you."

"That's lucky indeed. I just doubt I have what it takes to be a good fit. If nothing else, I'll be the most educated woman in the business."

"You're all shy at the beginning. You'll get over it once you see the money coming. Plus this education of yours, what good came out of it anyhow?"

"This is like asking me why I should be kind when ruthless people are the ones who rule the world. I'm kind because it makes me feel good and because..."

"And because it lets you sleep at night. I know, you all say that. The problem is what's happening when you wake up."

I had to admit she had a point. Longer we would have talked, I am sure more reasons she would have raised. But, this did not change the truth: I was an educated woman, which might not have meant much for her, but it meant the world for me. And while working never killed anyone, some sort of work might have killed me.

Once more, I could just imagine my mom's conversations:

"So, what is your daughter doing in Canada? Is she doing her master in law?"

"No, she's a stripper."

"Wow! That's interesting..."

"You tell me about it?"

So, for the sake of my mom and everyone else's, I refused. Too bad so sad, I was not given the option again. Must have been the age catching up with me.

Dora's Journal Notes

- *Your beauty can be used in many ways. Use it right!*
- *How you choose to make money says more about yourself than how much money you make.*

As if someone was determined to show me that all people are bad or just blind to my true qualities, the next disastrous job proposal came from a proud owner of a famous Torontonian cake store.

No bathtubs to install there, no poles to dance in the middle of the night, just some delicious cakes to serve and nice customers to take care of. Make no mistake, after my previous adventures, this was my dream job. However, there was just one itsy-bitsy problem: before getting paid, I had to prove my competencies in the area. At least, this guy believed I had some other skills as well, except those of an amazing stripper. So, I gave him credit.

But, after one month of working under a so-called "training program," I was not getting paid. It was blurry for everyone how much "training" I would still need and in what areas.

Was my smile not quite the right one? But if that was it, it was too late for my parents to change it and too expensive for a plastic surgeon to fix it.

Was my skirt not short enough or was it too short? I'm afraid the answer would have largely varied from customer to customer.

And so, unappreciated and broke, I quit this so called job.

Dora's Journal Notes

- *There are no verbal or written promises, just promises.*
- *Don't be shy or humble with your achievements! If you are, people will keep devaluing them, until there won't be anything left to be proud of.*

CHAPTER 10

EDUCATION SHOULD NOT BE DENIED TO THE ONES WHO WANT TO LEARN

Going back to school if you have money
Is more advisable than playing rummy.
But if you don't have it and ask the Gov
Good luck to you my dear dove

WHAT IS THE SECRET of a successful career in life?

First, I thought it is all about having the brains.

Then, somebody told me it is about having the right paper.

In the end, I found out that more than anything else, what you need is passion, lots of it.

For now though, I was stuck at the "right paper" phase. And, without much luck in finding a job, I jumped at the first opportunity of going back to school.

After getting a student grant from the government, I got accepted to a college to study for paralegal. I marked the day on the happy memories calendar and called Robert.

"Yay! I have news, Robert!"

"Sounds like big news to me."

"No big news, just baby steps. I'm still a baby, so what do you expect?"

"I'd say more of a babe than a baby."

"Ha! I got the grant! I'll study again!"

"Sweetie, that's great! You're great!"

And it was. Because the college was very far from where I was living, I had to move. And finding a new place was tricky. For an entire month, each day, I was knocking on doors, looking for a room to rent close to school, without any success. It was tiring, depressing and disheartening.

Finally, a week before the college started, an Indian guy offered me a room in a newly built house. But, when I went to see it, I found out the house was still under construction and so was the whole neighborhood. The nearest phone cabin was about fifteen-minutes walk, the bus stop about half an hour walk, as to the grocery shopping mall, it was yet to be built.

Lesson learned: If something sounds too good to be true, then it probably is.

But, when push comes to shove, there is not much you can do or you wouldn't do. So, all alone, I moved out to my spooky, haunted house.

Robert and I celebrated the event on the beach, well wrapped in our blankets, feeding a few Canadian geese, and hoping the worse was behind me.

My first week of school was fun, full of laughter, excitement and new hopes. But my happiness was short lived. The second week, a letter from the Government came:

"We are sorry to inform you, but a mistake has been made and the Government of Canada cannot offer you the grant. Please try again when you have been granted the Canadian citizenship."

"Yes, in about five years you mean!" I thought to myself. Then, I crashed.

With no money to continue the school, I was back to scratch. Back to...the truth is I had nothing to go back to. All the time I had invested in looking for a place, the money I have paid to move in, all my plans and efforts, all my hopes were once again, down the drain.

At two o'clock in the morning, at minus ten Celsius, I went walking around the house, with tears pouring down my face feeling hopeless and defeated.

Back home, I spent the rest of the night on the floor, blubbering like a child and wishing I would just die.

I had no money left, nowhere to go and no idea what to do next.

If there was a God, He was definitely either on holiday or on sick leave. His replacement, if He had one, was not doing a very good job.

To make everything worse, I got very sick. So sick that Robert decided to call the ambulance. After spending a whole night at the hospital, in a wheelchair, too weak to move or to talk, shaking with fever, the doctors finally found some time to see me. I had pneumonia.

Scared, I called my mom's cousin in Montreal hoping to stay with her for a few weeks until I would feel better. She listened to me, pretending to care, then she cut the conversation short and bluntly told me:

"My dear, it is your expedition, your adventure, and I do not want to have anything to do with it. Plus, I'm already late for a party and I cannot seem to find a pair of shoes to match my dress for tonight. Take care of yourself, dear."

And that was all.

This was my mom's cousin, always walking around in style, in her expensive, shiny clothes and always in too much of a hurry to stop and help someone else.

I will always remember her voice, her words and the way I felt. She was my own blood, the same one I use to write long letters to when she immigrated to Canada and she needed some encouragement.

This last blow hurt even more than any other. It made me think again of the meaning of family. For now, I might as well have been an orphan.

But, back from his too long holiday, God took pity on me and soon after my return from the hospital, an Indian girl moved in:

"My name is Simrin," she said with that lovely Indian accent which even Russell Peters would envy. "I heard what happened to you. Such a shame, really. But, you never know...things happen for a reason. I know what you need."

"Knowing is not the problem, dear. On the other hand, having is. I need a job and I need to get better," I said, sadly.

"You're right. But for now, we'll go together to an Indian wedding. It will be fun. We'll dance, get drunk and who knows what else..." Simrin replied, smiling provocative.

"Getting drunk and at an Indian wedding will be something new to me. As to that "what else" stuff, it is out of the question."

I could just imagine myself dressed in a pink sari, barefooted, with some Henna on my pale, white hands.

"So, it's all set."

"It is, if I'll make it till then."

"You're a tough cookie, you'll be more than fine."

"I'm not that greedy. Just fine will be quite enough for now. Or maybe not enough, but good enough."

So the next Saturday, here I was, dressed in a pink sari, to what was to be my first and probably my last Indian wedding. Although I didn't get drunk and because I was so sick I was barely able to walk, let alone to dance, I had fun watching the rice and other kinds of seeds thrown in the air and over each other, as a symbol of fertility and abundance. I learned that food eaten by hands is not bad, but it can become so when everyone else's hands are touching it. I smelled the curry over and over again, from the first word the Indian guy at the door said to me, to the last piece of clothing touching my skin. Other than that, I don't remember much of it.

"You must be tired and something tells me a bit hungry too," Simrin told me once we got back home. "You don't like curry much, do you?"

"I think I'm still at the first phase, trying to get used to its smell. At least, I could easily tell an Indian from a non-Indian, even blindfolded."

She laughed:

"True. You know what they say, you are what you eat."

"With the Indian version being: you smell like what you eat."

"Admit it: it's cheap perfume!"

"With the emphasis on cheap!"

"I love your humor, even the cynic side of it. I'll make us a cup of tea and some tasty sandwich. You don't look well tonight. I think I'll sleep next to you, just in case you need something."

"If only all the Indians were like you, Simrin," I answered, grateful for her willingness to help me.

"And all the Romanians like you, Dora."

"But we know they are not," we both said in one voice.

For the next few weeks, Simrin took care of me, like a devoted mother will do for her child. Each night, she made sure she put a smile on my face, listened to my worries, tried to give me advice and prayed with me, for me. From a stranger, she became my family and my mom's cousin from family became a stranger.

For years and years I hated my mom's cousin for not helping me and for destroying my trust in what a family is. All those days when I was shivering with fever under the blankets, I was imagining her in one of her shopping frolics, smiling and laughing, hiding behind her beautiful appearance a heart of ice, deceiving and mean. For years, I wished one day she would feel what I felt, she would need someone to help her and everyone would turn their backs on her.

But then, one day, I stopped. I buried her like you bury a stranger, with no tears in your eyes and no memories left behind. She became a no one for me, a stranger, same as I was once a no one to her, a stranger. I refused to let hate poison my heart and I chose to let only the love and appreciation for my Indian girl fill my days.

I replaced the bad memories of my mom's cousin with the happy ones with Simrin.

I learned to forgive, but never to forget. Because forgiving sets you free, while forgetting gives others another chance to hurt you.

With Robert and Simrin by my side, I started again to look for jobs and rooms for rent in a more populated area.

Like a Phoenix, I was determined to rise from the ashes.

Dora's Journal Notes

- *If the road starts being bumpy, tighten your seat belt, look ahead, and keep driving.*
- *Where there is a way down, you can always find a way up.*
- *There may be times when the action itself does not say much about us, but the circumstance in which it is done says everything.*
- *Memories are a bit like your clothes. Only the best ones are worth keeping.*

CHAPTER 11

A CHINESE ROOMMATE, THE PHILOSOPHY OF A NATION

Your house is your castle,
Some might wisely say,
But how to find the right one
Nobody can say!

MOVING IN WITH A ROOMMATE is like buying a lottery ticket. You never know how it will turn out.

However, no matter the outcome, I've always found it to be an opportunity to grow.

I learned new habits, new smells, like curry, and sometimes I even made new friends, like Simrin. Having roommates of different nationalities opened my eyes to new cultures, stirred my curiosity, immersed me into others' ways of being, and exposed me to experiences I couldn't get as a tourist. It taught me to respect every person, each story, and every culture, and to realize how much we can all learn from each other.

For an Eastern European girl like me, Chinese and Indians were particularly interesting, so different and so exotic. I had never used chopsticks, never heard of dumplings or curry, and all I knew about them was from books.

After my pleasant experience with Simrin, I found a room for rent with a Chinese lady, Ning.

Ning was what we may call a woman with a mission. She worked around the clock and everything she did followed a strict plan. She did not let her feelings, assuming she had any, stand in her way, and getting pregnant was not an exception to the rule.

"Why you cannot come over tonight?" she said to her boyfriend over the phone, one Monday night "You don't understand. Saturday will be too late. I'm ovulating. You must come now. It won't take long," she assured him.

And she was right. It never took long. He went to her bedroom and before I knew it, he was out the door.

"Time is money," Ning used to say to me.

"Is it anything else, other than money, Ning?"

"What else? There is nothing else."

And for her, there wasn't.

She saved each penny, spared none, and monitored each deal on the market, whether it was for elastic bands or for rice. Money was her only and constant obsession and if having lots of it meant working day and night, she was ready to do it.

Wearing the same sturdy pair of shoes on all seasons, she was the retail business nightmare and the shame of all the women on the planet. No dapper wardrobe for her. All her clothes, including the underwear, were self-made in her room each night after work.

But, to really know Ning, you had to go with her for a drive.

"Ning, you're driving like a true Chinese," I told her, seeing her facial muscles tighten, her steady look, and her hands grabbing the steering wheel as if it was a lifesaving device.

"What do you mean like a Chinese?"

"It means bad, terribly bad."

"Chinese not good at driving cars, Chinese good at driving people," she said in her broken English.

"If by driving people you mean driving them insane, then you are right, very right," I teased her.

Although it was hidden deep enough for anyone to have a chance to find it, Ning had her unique sense of humor. She exercised it on my birthday card: "Do not keep bags full of garbage inside the house, keep the fridge clean, wash off the bread from kitchen table. I bought you a hair product. Do not color anything else than your hair. And please, do not leave me turned on, Ning." Knowing what an electricity hog Ning was, I assumed she referred to the lights. Who could ask for more from a birthday card?

But Ning was a good-hearted lady. At midnight, when I was back from work, frozen, exhausted, and hungry, she used to wait for me with a bowl of rice and a cup of hot tea. On Christmas, as a present, she made pajamas for me.

Like Simrin, Ning was there for me when I needed a shoulder to cry on, which, truth be told, was often the case. Her advice was always the same: work hard and have patience. She was not an emotional woman, but a practical one. With her, you knew what you got. She meant every word she said and kept every promise she made. She was a friend whom you could count on.

What I liked the most about Ning was that she never pretended to be more than what she was: a simple, hardworking Chinese immigrant in search for a simple, but better life, forged by her and her only, without taking advantage of anyone. For these reasons, in my eyes, she was much more of a lady than my mom's cousin would ever be.

I lived with Ning and her quirky habits until, after multiple, carefully timed, trial and error "experiments," she got pregnant, moved in with her boyfriend, and decided to sell her apartment.

I always wondered what happened to her over the years. I could just imagine her with kids, a husband, working harder than ever, at a huge sewing machine, making underwear and pajamas for her whole family.

Dora's Journal Notes

- *When one is in distress, some will offer a bowl of rice, others a long lecture and the rest will turn around. Be the one who offers a bowl of rice.*
- *You stop living when you stop challenging yourself.*
- *Only when you will respect others' journeys, you will be ready to start your own.*

CHAPTER 12

NIGHT WATCH AT A HOTEL, LOULOU - THE WILD CHICKEN AND LINGERIE'S MYSTERIES

Being back in the workforce was always "fun,"
Knowing I was there for the long run,
But with little money in and lots going out
I started to feel a little bit of a doubt.
Maybe I should've been a bloody lawyer,
Pompous and rich, rather than a penniless Tom
Sawyer!

LIVING WITH SUCH a penny pincher and workaholic like Ning left me with no other choice than to match her closely.

In no time, I found not one job, but four: sales person for an electronics store, dishwasher associate in a family restaurant, receptionist at a dental office, and sales person at a lingerie store. Yes, it was before the global financial crises. Before congratulating and starting to envy me, let me tell you that they were all located in different parts of the city, and the closest one was an hour away.

Greedy, I took them all and let the fun begin.

Suddenly, my week did not have enough days, my days did not have enough hours, and as for the hours, they too, did not have enough minutes. I forgot to sleep, to eat, to walk, or to talk. Despite working like stevedores, all I made was barely enough to pay for my rent and groceries. However, what mattered to me was there: I felt free, with no one to answer to except myself, and no other expectations to fulfill except my own.

At the electronics store, with no idea about the products or the slightest interest in learning about them, I was about to win the championship for the most clueless salesperson ever by a mile.

"Do you know what sells better?" my manager asked me one day.

"I think some knowledge would help," I replied.

"Maybe, but it's your smile that will close the deal."

And since that day, there were only two moments when I was fully aware of being an employee and not a customer: firstly, when after eight hours of standing, my legs were all pins and needles, and secondly, when at the end of the day, I had to sweep the floor. The rest of the time, I was busy chattering away and joking with the customers coming into the store, listening to their stories, their worries and making some new friends. So, the smile did work. Things to remember: sometimes, even the boss is right.

Even at the lingerie store, I felt a bit of a stranger. I am sure any men could easily understand my feelings. However, I was a woman, but apparently not womanly enough.

"You'd think that should be easy. A bra, some panties, sexy pajamas, no brainer! But no. Choosing one, wearing one, taking one off, it all gets more and more complicated," I told Robert over lunch.

"You tell me about it," he replied, amused.

"First it's the bra: front clasp or back clasp, underwire or not, push-up or just natural, cotton or bouncy, lacy, gels or foams, red is hot or black is hotter, white is boring, but pink is silly and so on. Then, it's the panties: high rise, low rise or granny-panty, boy-cut, no-cut or high-cut, cotton, nylon or silky, firm, extra firm or loose and so on."

"But the choice is simple: the bra, if you must and only if you must: front clasp, no push ups, no wires, no gels, no foams and who cares about the color, by the time you finish the undressing part, it gets dark anyway."

"So no more deceiving: what you see is what you get," I concluded.

"Yup. Now, the panties: for high pressure, low rise; for low pressure, high-rise; for no pressure, the granny ones. That cut thing sounds dangerous. No cut please, will ya?"

"Soon, we'll all be in dire need of some lingerie dictionary."

"Preferably with full pictures attached," he said with a spark in his eyes.

"Of a granny?"

"No way! Then maybe just with some of the pictures attached."

"Discrimination!" I shouted.

"Just basic marketing."

"As to the pajamas, why anyone would buy one of those silky fully see through pinky ones, beats me. If you want to make a statement, then you'd better just present yourself in all your naked splendor. At least, you'd save some precious time," the practical side of me said.

"It's called teasing, my dear."

"Teasing, but no pleasing. All show, no go."

"You are a woman of action."

"And satisfaction. So many choices and all this time, no one thinks of men. What do they want? How would they prefer spending the time? Figuring out how to take them off and looking like some silly nerds or diving right into it?"

"If only all the women thought like you..."

"I know. The lingerie stores will go bankrupt."

"But the condom ones will flourish, eh?"

"I doubt it," I said, smiling. "Shall I start? Extra sensitive, ultra-sensitive, orange, blue, black, cinnamon, mint, cherry, small, large, extra-large, regular, thick, wet, dry, ribs, bumps, studs, and it goes on."

"Life is complicated."

"We surely make it so."

As the "dishwasher associate" at the family restaurant, I felt ... oh well, how should I put it? Happy, content, miserable? None of it, really, just soaking wet while wearing oversized boots and trying to maneuver an oversized hose. Day after day, I was hanging on the owner's promise that I would get promoted to waitress if I did a good job. However, whatever standards I was up against, I must have failed all of them.

The most influential one was revealed to me one day when his male instincts took over and he made the indecent proposal: after hours, we could have some fun time when his wife was not around.

"Too bad," I said, "I quite fancy your wife."

And so, all I ever got promoted to was manager in charge of more and more dirty dishes.

As a receptionist at the dental office, I would have been bored to death if not for the love affair between the dentist and his mistress. Each week, I was entertained watching a new episode from the hide-and-seek series. I figured it must be terribly stressful to have a mistress on the side.

So, if you get one, take my advice and make sure she or he is very good at whatever you miss.

Dora's Journal Notes

- *Forget everything, but never forget your smile.*
- *No matter how simple a job is, you can always find an employee for whom it is complicated.*
- *Any team needs a leader, but the problem is that every player thinks he should be the one.*
- *Between wisdom and stupidity there is only one difference: one knows when the time is right, the other believes any time is right.*
- *Nowadays, everyone wants to have something big. I settle on the heart.*

As I was a bit slow or maybe just too resilient, it took me a few months to give up on spending two hours on the road just so I could work for four. But, better late than never, like they say. And so, I resigned and started to work one job only as a parking attendant at one of the most luxurious malls in Toronto.

This "high end" position proved to require all sorts of skills and talents, from being a good listener to a worldwide entertainer for wealthy women decrying their terrible fate, while kissing their freshly groomed dogs. Finding ways to cheer them up and show them life is beautiful required a lot of imagination, patience, and humor. I had to be good at being their clown for as long as they wanted, or they would transform their pathetic plight into an insatiable desire to see me fired.

I can vividly remember one particular scene: she was tall, slim, blond, with blue eyes. Alluring in her Gucci dress, Madam was walking around on her high heel Jimmy Choo shoes, carrying Loulou, her dear chook. But Loulou was not happy. The perfume was not its favorite, and the mall not its chosen playground. And so, Loulou escaped. And in frenzy, it started running around the parking lot, facing the terrible danger of being hit by a car.

"Do something!" Madam screamed at me. "Can't you see Loulou is in grave danger?"

"And what would you like me to do? Run after a chicken? Put her on a leash," I replied bluntly.

"A leash? On Loulou's fragile neck? Maybe on yours! You are a savage!" she shouted at me, horrified by my suggestion.

"Is it organic chicken?" I went on.

"And what would be the relevance of it *now*?" she asked with her eyes getting bigger and bigger.

"Particularly *now* I think it's important. You see, I'm only used to organic chicken," I replied in a serious tone.

"Phew! Animal!" she yelled at me.

"Animal indeed!" I concluded.

Then, all hell broke loose. In less than five minutes, the entire parking lot become a scene taken right from a comedy movie, with the main protagonist being nothing more than a damn restless chicken. The cars were honking, the chook was speeding, and Madam took her Jimmy Choo shoes off and started running after the chicken, while I started to chase them both. The security guards were alerted and more or less everyone was actively involved in keeping the chick safe.

"Break, break, I need a break!" I wanted to scream at Loulou. But I could barely breathe.

And, after we all got tired, Loulou finally got tired too. Reluctantly, he accepted its fate and reclaimed its prime spot in Madam's arms, who was filled with joy and relief.

"Loulou, my baby. Give mama a kiss!"

And this was the true story of a rich beautiful lady and her disobedient pet, Loulou, the wild chicken.

Dora's Journal Notes

- *Happiness does not come from what we have or from having what we want, but from appreciating what it is given to us in each moment.*
- *Be a good sport! Treat each fall as an opportunity: with courage, determination, and hope.*
- *Between optimism and pessimism, I choose the first. It seems to me the only logical choice as pessimism takes you nowhere while optimism takes you somewhere, the worst being back to nowhere.*

Did you ever dream of snapping a shot with some celebrity? Or maybe getting one of those Top Hundred

World Richest people to fall in love with you, just so in the end you can refuse him for his lack of manners?

I did.

"What better way for all this to happen than working in a luxury hotel?" I said to Robert.

"Maybe just staying at one, eh?" he suggested.

"That comes after, dear."

"As long as it comes, it's fine with me. And what job would you like to have there? You have no experience in this industry."

"Like I had a lot of it in the electronic business, or the plumbing one, or all the rest. I'll find a job there."

"As what? As a cleaning lady?"

"You sound upset. Better to be a cleaning lady at the Ritz than a cleaning lady at some no-name mall around the corner, don't you think?"

"Better to be a lawyer in your own country than a cleaner in someone else's."

"So, this is what's bothering you. I'll get there. You know I will."

"You will, but only if you stop devaluing yourself! If you stop acting like something you're not! You wanted to know why I'm pissed off, now you know," Robert exclaimed, infuriated.

I knew he was right. But, for now, I needed the money.

A few days later, I started to work as a receptionist, the second smiling or grumpy face, depending on my day, after the bellboy.

The job wouldn't have been so bad if, on my second week, I wouldn't have been "promoted" to what I hated the most: night shifts. Even worse, the policy of the hotel was that everyone at the front desk had to work standing up. During the late hours of the night, when most of the guests were sound asleep in their hopefully comfortable beds and only one or two were passing by, standing like a soldier made no sense whatsoever. Nevertheless, it was the rule, and the consequences were quite predictable: my back was sore and the pain in my legs was excruciating. My body soon started to fail me, and I became a ghost, barely able to drag myself to work each night. In the wee hours of the morning, back home, all I wanted was to lie on the hard floor and cry. This was my glamorous hotel job.

On Christmas Eve, when I saw the house full of people partying, while half-awake I was getting ready for another shift, I burst into tears.

Maybe aspiring to be more than a cleaning lady was a mistake. After all, the cleaners were the only ones who were never called for an emergency. They worked only day shifts and could sit down, lie down, and make themselves a cup of tea whenever they pleased.

Or maybe Robert was right. This hunting for jobs without having a clear idea in my mind of what I would like to find, without giving myself a break to pause and to think, this continuous fight for survival, was taking me nowhere.

"What do you think will happen to me, Robert?"

"What do I think? It won't happen what I think or what your family or even your foes want. It will happen only what you believe it will happen. Same as till now."

"How can you say that? I never wanted any of these. I never wanted this job. I just need this job. I need to support myself."

"Ever since you landed you needed the money. This did not turn you into a stripper, when you were offered to become one. Why should you now turn yourself into a ghost? Quit and move on, like you always did. The future will take care of itself. You just be careful with your thoughts."

Said and done. After six months of mental and physical torture, despite having no savings, I mustered all my courage and quit. The first thing I planned to do was to sleep all day and all night for as long as I could.

Dora's Journal Notes

- *Don't envy anyone. There will always be parts of their lives, known or unknown, you could not put up with.*
- *No job is worth your health.*
- *Any decision that brings you relief is good.*

CHAPTER 13

FRIENDSHIP AND ITS PERKS

Friendships are in times of need,
What love is in times of breed.
When it's long lasting and true,
It's the best thing that can happen to you!

ROBERT, THE MAN I MET a few hours after my landing in Canada, who helped me to find my first apartment and watched over me ever since, was neither rich nor handsome.

He was a common Canuck working his way through life, with no tertiary education, a bit frumpy and short, always tardy, and all over the place. But his heart was beautiful, helping everyone from the last beggar met at the subway to the closest friend met in kindergarten. That's not to say he was naïve. He had a knack for people, could tell the bad ones from the good ones, the sincere from the crooks, after just a few minutes of conversation. And he was rarely wrong.

He judged people not by their clothes, their cars, or their bank accounts. What he was looking for in a person was far beyond what money can buy or what one might have today and lose tomorrow. He was looking for genuine kindness.

Looking back, in Romania I wouldn't have had the curiosity to know him better. Well hidden in my own upper social class, guarded all around by preconceptions, I used to judge people by their formal education or their lack of it.

But my life in Canada taught me more than that. Here, the richest man could choose to drive a Honda while the poor one might have saved his whole life to proudly now drive a Mercedes, or the cleaning guy at the mall could have been a doctor with a PhD from a country ravaged by war, whose studies were not recognized.

None of those aspects changed who those people really were, what they knew, or what they had.

Robert was a true man and not knowing him would have been entirely my loss.

For all the confidence he had in me when no one else had, he was and remained my hero, my guardian angel.

Thanks to him, I survived all the storms, I found the strength to follow my dreams and to never kneel. He was my armor, my torch, my refuge.

And to make it all complete, he was the funniest man I've ever met, living day by day by the motto, "Seven days without laughter makes one weak."

It was Sunday afternoon when, after crying about my fate all day long, he came over, accompanied by his unmistakable, unflagging good cheer.

"I know the best way to see that perfect smile on you again," he proclaimed.

"Why do I feel scared of asking what that is?"

"I don't know. Why do you, eh?"

"Because I know you?"

"Do you, missy?" he said, cracking a mischievous smile. "Get dressed; we're goin' to the Human Body Exhibition."

"Where?"

"To the Human Body Exhibition. Haven't you ever wondered what's inside this little head of yours? I always do," he said, amused. "I wanna know you inside out and then I can die happy." He paused for a few seconds. "Although I might prefer the 'live happily ever after' version."

"You're joking. You're always joking. Can you ever be serious?"

"Can I or do I want to?"

"I've got a hunch the answer to both is no. At least stop laughing all the time. People will think I'm tickling you."

"You do, you tickle my fancy. All the time. Plus if I want to have a laugh, I'll have to be the first one to make others laugh," he said on a serious tone. "Now, you have five minutes to get dressed. After that, whatever you don't have on you, stays home. And the five minutes start...NOW!"

"All right already. We'll go."

And so we went to see this famous exhibition, which showcased preserved human bodies that had been dissected to display bodily systems. At first, the idea seemed crazy: I wasn't a fan of horror movies and I wasn't planning on being a surgeon. However, after an all-day session with skulls, skeletons, open veins, and pubic bones, I came home and looked in the mirror and thought I looked gorgeous and on top of that, guess what, I was alive too. What better reasons to celebrate and start a new week smiling?

Robert also remained famous in my personal *Guinness* book of records as the fastest guy, running not away from me, but after me. I was flying to Romania without telling anyone. He was resourceful enough to find out the day, but not enough to find out the time. After a long honking battle with the traffic, one hour before the plane took off, he arrived at the airport without a clue where he could find me. He shared my picture around, asking desperately if anyone had seen me. Right before entering the security gates, I heard my name called:

"Dora is asked to come at check-in counter number two."

Once, twice, three times. I was a missing and wanted person!

Suddenly I could see him, rolling like a snowball, kneeling in front of me, trying to catch his breath.

"Have a safe flight, sweetie. Canada will miss you. But I'll miss you even more." Then he handed me a bunch of five dollars calling cards. "A call to know you're good will be nice! Any day, at any time!"

After the expected sobbing episode, I entered the security gates. Then, I turned around and said, while tears came pouring down my face:

"You're one of a kind, my precious!"

"If I am, then stop making me run like a yo-yo, missy."

"There comes a time when we all show our true colors."

"What? I'll get you for that one."

"Be my guest, precious," I responded giving him a big smile, just before turning around and disappearing behind the gates.

His only fault in my eyes was that he was a bit of a night owl, but like always, he had an amusing explanation for it.

"You'll get wrinkles from not sleeping properly," I scolded him.

"Wrinkles are a sign of wisdom, people let you sit down on the bus, listen to you more carefully, are understanding when you're forgetful, they..."

"Stop making fun of everything! Promise me you will go to sleep early tonight."

"And who will protect my family when the monsters come at night to eat us all, eh?" he said with a whining voice.

"All in the name of love, poor you!"

"Poor me? What are you talkin' about? I'm not poor, I have you! This makes me the richest man alive."

"Or the dumbest!" I laughed.

We have spent one of the most beautiful Christmases together. In Quebec, surrounded by snow, ski slopes, outdoor hot tubs, going dog sledding and discovering snowmobiling, Christmas was the way it is supposed to be: white, cold, with Santa arriving on his famous sleigh with reindeers, with his red nose sticking out predicting temperatures well below zero. We waited for him next to the fireplace, looking out the window at the snowfall, in warm cozy pajamas, drinking hot chocolate, and listening to carols in a beautiful small chalet up in the mountains.

That Christmas day was magical. At almost minus forty degrees Celsius, there was no one around. The snow was up our waist, the rivers were frozen, and the sky was clear. Everything was still and all I could hear were our own footsteps cutting pathways through the untouched snow. The forest was all ours and with each step, I could feel myself falling under its spell.

Such a blissful, needed fall...

"I love you!" he suddenly said to me.

"I know," I replied looking away, unable to meet his eyes. I cared about him more than anyone; he was my best friend, my only one, there was nothing I would not have done for him. He was part of me. But, I did not love him, at least not the way I knew he wanted me to, not the way he deserved to be. The spark was never there and it was nothing I could do to change that. And I treasured our friendship too much to lie to him.

Like he could read my mind, he continued:

"No reason to feel guilty. Love is rarely, if ever, a conscious choice. I did not plan on lovin' you, same as I cannot plan to stop lovin' you."

"Can we still be friends?"

"For sure. You owe me at least that, missy."

"I owe you more than that. I just wish I could give it to you. It's just that..."

"Stop here! Justifying your decision is not your style. And justifying your feelings sounds even less like you. The moment when you chose to confide in me, to share your dreams and fears with me, in that moment you already gave me the best of you. Loving you made me happy, being next to you made me happy and seeing you grow made me ever happier. Seeing all the other guys roaming around you, hmmm, not very happy," he laughed. "In my wildest dreams, I imagine myself making love to you."

"Someone has got the dreaming part right."

"Yep! However, the reality seems to be a bit of an issue."

"Think of it like that: they may all want me, some might even have me, but sooner or later they might be gone. But you, my friend, will always remain."

"Tortured for life! That sounds promising."

"Stop it! You make me sound like an awful person."

"Not awful. Just tantalizing, freakin' beautiful. Outside and inside. Not your fault, I know. Let's walk back. We'll freeze if we'll stay here longer."

"Love you."

"I love you too, sweetie," he said giving me a kiss on the forehead. "More than you'll ever know."

Although he never became my lover, he was and remained my lifetime best friend, the most amazing, loyal, wise, and funniest guy, with a heart made of pure gold.

Dora's Journal Notes

- *While some might be good at talking about love, others might just show you what it means.*
- *True friendship is built in time of need and celebrated each day.*
- *If you are extraordinary today it's only because someone extraordinary believed in you. It's your turn to do the same.*
- *Without lovers we might survive, but without friends we will crumble.*
- *Never let a true friend go. You might never find another.*
- *For women, being close means telling you everything you don't really want to know.*

CHAPTER 14

WHEN KINDNESS DOES THE TRICK

When working hard is all you do,
But no one seems to care for you;
When things keep piling up ahead,
Despite working till you drop dead,

Just take a step, a wide step back
And try to be less of a maniac,
Open your arms and heart and mind,
Believe in you and just be kind!

"TODAY MARKS THREE YEARS since I left my homeland," I said to myself on a beautiful day of spring while coming out of the subway. "Three years since I came to Toronto hoping to find a job, to go back to school, and slowly build a whole new life from scratch."

And what did you do? my inner voice replied, *move at least five times, hold at least ten different jobs, and cry at least twice every day.*

"I know. It seems the harder I work, the fewer rewards I get out of it. I'm tired of climbing a mountain that keeps hiding its peak from me like Fata Morgana keeps hiding her face from tired travelers. Robert is right. Better to be a lawyer in my own country than a cleaner in someone else's."

You mean it's better to give up than stay and fight.

"It's a lot of wisdom in giving up too."

And a lot of fear that some call wisdom as well.

I probably would have continued to beat myself up if not for the old homeless street musician playing a violin. It was gypsy music, and it reminded me of home. I loved that music. Every day as I walked by, it put a smile on my face, took a wrinkle off my forehead, and gave me a glitter in my eyes.

"People like him, artists, make the world a better place to be," I said to myself, feeling a strong impulse to give him my twenty dollars.

At first it seemed silly, but more I thought about it, more it felt like the right thing to do. No struggle, no disappointment, no humiliation should stop us be humble, compassionate, and goodhearted.

I reached my pockets and handed him the bill. He smiled and thanked me. It was the most genuine smile I saw in months.

I did not want to know how he ended up on the streets. It was not my place to judge him. The last three years taught me that no matter how high up you are, no matter how secure you think your life is, one day everything can change. Sometimes it might be your fault, sometimes not. It does not matter. All that matters is you still have a heart, you are still a human being, and you need compassion, understanding, and support more than ever before.

I was not doing it for him to praise me and I expected nothing in return.

My pockets were empty and my mind troubled, but my heart was still generous and pure. And as long as it remained as such, I knew, sooner or later, everything else would fall into place.

The music kept playing in tone with the wind howling through the subway tunnel.

That day, I promised myself to give something away each day: sometimes an hour of my time or a piece of advice, other times money or food, and each day a smile for someone less lucky than me. I promised to be kind.

The following week, I found a well-paying nine-to-five job in a real estate office, and my employers became my close friends. With a secure job, I could finally move into a nice apartment, all alone, and buy the furniture I dreamed of.

You might say it was a coincidence and you might be right. However, I chose to believe that it was the universe's response to my kindness: give and you shall receive.

Dora's Journal Notes

- *True kindness does not wait to be asked, does not have a particular recipient, does not ask for reasons nor expects anything in return.*
- *Keep your goals constant, but always be willing to change your approach.*
- *It is your mind that turns obstacles into dead ends.*

CHAPTER 15

A FEW GENUINE ADVANTAGES OF LIVING ALONE

After a Chinese roommate
And a lesbian kind of date,
After cockroaches roaming free,
Never in hoards of less than three,
Moving in a clean, nice place,
By myself in all that space,
Felt a little bit surreal,
No more trial by ordeal!

"Finally! My own place! I am free to do whatever I want, with whoever I want, whenever I want, Robert!"

"Finally no more roommates, naked or half naked, alluring or disgusting, lesbian, straight, or whatever is out there," Robert said, excited for me.

"Won't my life be boring now?"

"You mean finally a bit of normality! I was getting worn out by all these ups and downs of yours."

"I was just getting fit! I promise no more of these ups and downs from now on! However, I cannot promise other ups and downs won't take their place," I said, blowing him a kiss.

"About time."

"True," I responded, thinking that for more than four years now, I did not have a real boyfriend.

"Well done, sweetie. You came a long way. One dream accomplished. And, 'cause I know how much you love gardening and hate cut flowers, here you go," he handed me a pot full of herbs wrapped around in red, yellow, and blue paper, the colors of the Romanian flag.

"Is that all?" I pretended to be disappointed.

"And a card. As for pinching your sexy *postérieur*, this comes later. Open the card and read it out loud! That's an order!"

"A unicorn on the cover?! Hmm... '*May all your dreams come true... especially the weird ones. From one dreamer to another. Te pup. Robert.*'"

Te pup was the first Romanian word I taught him, and it means kiss you.

"Then do it. Make the words count," I said, giving him the cheek.

"You're the best," he said gently.

"I know. The best around here. Out there, in the big world, that's a different story," I joked. "Let's cook something. I am starving!"

"Not sure about that. Last time you cooked, I ate and flossed at the same time."

"What do you mean?"

"You know what I mean; your hair can't seem to resist the temptation of gettin' in your tasty dishes."

I blushed. He continued:

"No need to be embarrassed. You taste good! Now, I could use some cool refreshing pop before you make a total shambles of your kitchen."

We laughed.

When the time came for some serious renovations, sitting comfortably on my queen-sized bed, I recalled the times when I was sleeping on an inflatable single mattress in that awful bachelor apartment which back then I called home. So much had changed since that day and I made it all happen. Sometimes I had tears in my eyes, other times a smile on my face, but passion, determination, and faith were always with me. Red must have been my color. And so, I let my imagination go wild and bought my first couch. Red. Taken by itself, the event shouldn't have meant much. After all, everyone has a couch, be it red, black, or white. For me, though, after immigrating with two suitcases and without much money, that red couch was more than just a couch. It was a symbol. To create the perfect set up for a sinful night, even if all alone, I painted the wall behind it in strong bright yellow.

After my whole apartment was colorful enough to compete with a flashy Lorikeet and still win, I stopped. I took a long bath accompanied by a glass of Sangria and let Carl Orff's masterpiece, *Carmina Burana*, play its magic.

After such a long struggle, one by one, my wishes were starting to come true. I had the world by the tail and no one could have convinced me otherwise.

Dora's Journal Notes

- *If you cannot find contentment in solitude, you will never find it in the crowd.*

CHAPTER 16

CUBA: LA DOLCE VITA

Travel far and travel wide,
Leave your worries far behind,
Royal Palms, a strong Mojito,
A cigar or a burrito,
Hemingway and Bienvenido.

CUBA! My first holiday in years!

"You'll love it here!" the lady next to me assured me on our way to the hotel. "I come here every year! You know, it's the people!"

"*It's the people...* I wonder what that means. Are nations indeed so different from each other? Or is each person different from the other?"

"Both."

Looking out the window, I couldn't see much: just royal palm trees, the Cuban national symbol and the sea...

"*Bienvenida a Cuba!*" the lady at the reception said, handing me the key to my room with one hand and with the other a freshly prepared Mojito.

"Thank you," I responded, listening to the beautiful piano music played by a dark skinned guy.

The warm Caribbean breeze and the humidity in the air were making me feel dizzy, a pleasurable dizziness. One after another I could just feel my worries melting away.

The room was simple, the furniture old, the TV small, but there was something cozy about the whole place.

I turned the TV on: "*Guantanamera,...*"

"*Guantanamera...,*" I started singing along, dancing in the mirror. "Oh, that feels good! I love Cuba!"

And from that day till the last day, my feelings have not changed.

Next morning, I decided to see Havana and looked for a touring companion. After meeting a curious Canadian guy about fifty years of age who had to ask his father's permission to get out of the resort without much success, I thought it was all in vain. But then I made a Cuban friend: she was the only person at the car rental office. Without thinking twice, she simply said to me:

"You want to go to Havana and have no one to go with? No problem. I close the office and we go."

"Right..." For a second my mind could not process the information: job, responsibility, the one and only person in the rental office. *Hello, are you taking me for a fool?* She couldn't just leave the office. She must have been joking. But she was not.

And, there we were, two women in an old American car, heading towards La Habana.

"*Guantanamera... guajira, Guantanamera.* Sing with me!" she shouted while trying desperately to dance, talk, and wave to the other drivers all at the same time.

"*Guantanamera, guajira, Guantanamera,*" I hummed along, knowing the song by now.

"You, Canadians, don't sing much, don't dance much, and don't make love much. Here, we live to love, smoke cigars, dance salsa and drink Mojitos."

"We don't have much time. It's life, always standing in our way."

"I know, you trade time for a bigger TV, a fancy car, and an expensive restaurant."

"It's a bit more complicated than that."

"It's as complicated as you make it, amiga. But anyway, it's a far too beautiful day to talk about those things. By the end of your holiday, you'll understand what I mean."

"Tell me about Cuba. It seems such a peaceful place, but also a bit sad, is it?"

"Sad? No one is sad here. Maybe just the ones thinking the grass is always greener on the other side. But, those ones will always be sad wherever they go. Happiness comes from here," she said, pointing to her heart.

I looked at her a bit envious, a bit curious, and anxious to hear her story.

"In Cuba, the houses might not look like much, but they are ours! Furniture, like everything else, is hard to find. But when we do find it, oh, isn't that a happy moment! Even my bed must be a hundred years old. But it's a sturdy one, wood made. It has seen a lot!" She smiled.

When she said that, I suddenly remembered a seminar about mattresses I went to. The guy was trying to convince us they need to be changed every few years because of the dust mites multiplying in our beds each day. Then, a friend of mine jumped in: "Hey, at least someone is having sex in my bed." We all laughed at the reality of his words.

As she could read my mind, my Cuban lady continued:

"I love fast and furious love making! In the morning, it's the best wake-up call! You see, in Cuba, people are in love with love, with life, with one another! I love my husband and he loves me, so why not, I say? Use it or you lose it, isn't it how it goes? So, what about you? How many times in one night?"

"Me? Hmm…I'm single."

"Single? So young and beautiful and single? What do you do all day?"

"Not much. Just work."

"Work? This is what you all do there. Slaves hiding behind illusions. Isn't *that* sad?"

"Perhaps…What village is this?" I asked, showing her some terribly run-down buildings, with broken windows, from which people were coming in and out.

"Village? That's Havana, love! The old Havana! C'mon, we'll go visit a cigar factory and if you'd like, we can take a ride in a yellow Coco Taxi. It will be fun!"

We spent the whole day walking around Old Havana. With its old streets and buildings, its American cars from the '40s and '50s and its pharmacies, which still sold potions in jars instead of manufactured pills, Havana was a place of the past. But its crumbling Colonial buildings still charmed me, just in a different way than the modern towers of New York would; they reminded me that it is just a question of time before everything eventually becomes dust.

At night, she dragged me into a small local restaurant. It was hot and crowded.

Here, wrapped in the shroud of the mystery given by their latest cigar, Cuban men must fall asleep listening to the sound of rumba, Celia Cruz and dreaming of curvaceous women in colorful Spanish dresses. What a life," I said.

"Then, in the morning, they come home. And you know what's happening in the morning..." she responded hinting at our earlier discussion. "Let's drink! For you, for love..."

"And love making!" I added.

"May be no day without."

"And for Cuban people, for their open heart, humor, kindness, and wisdom! For their spirit!"

"For you my friend and for a life that matters!"

We drank Mojito after Mojito. And I was happy.

That day was a life lesson. It showed me life should and can be enjoyed even by those who drive old crappy cars, live in tiny rundown houses with no windows left intact, have a survival job if any, and, on special occasions, dine out at some decrepit family restaurant on the side of the road.

Cubans were not whiners, but fighters. They loved life, looked for what was positive in it, and forgot their sorrow in the arms of a lover, a smoke of a good cigar, a glass of Mojito, or the rhythm of rumba. For them, dancing was more natural than walking, smoking cigars better than talking, and smiling came always before asking. In my eyes, Cuban people were living the essence of what the rest of us merely preach.

They knew how to live and my friend was no different.

Her prayer became my prayer:

God, I ask you to give me wisdom to understand my man, enough love to forgive him, patience with his anger and frustrations, because God, if you give me strength, I will kill him.

Dora's Journal Notes

- *When you have all that makes you happy around you, look no further.*
- *You might chase the American dream in America, but you might find it somewhere else.*
- *The best job is the one that feeds you and still lets you enjoy life.*
- *The size of a place is less important than the company that comes with it.*

CHAPTER 17

PERU: MAN-MADE AND GOD-MADE ISLANDS

*When we're too close we cannot see
Or we see all that we shouldn't see,
That's why perspective is well advised
And a trip far away highly prized!*

AFTER SPENDING FIVE YEARS in Canada, I felt I reached a plateau.

Maybe I was looking too much in the wrong direction, thinking too much about the wrong things, or feeling too much for the wrong people.

Maybe there was nothing there for me to learn and to love, nothing left to excite me or inspire me.

Whatever the reasons were, deep inside, I did not feel I belonged there.

Having said that, I had no idea what to do next. To find out, I had to travel again, somewhere far enough, different enough to detach myself from my daily worries and fears. There, in peace and harmony, I knew the answer would reveal itself.

The question was where.

In search of serenity, Buddha, or the secrets of Kama Sutra, some go to India. I doubted contentment could be found in meditation; I still had lots to learn from Christ before moving on to Buddha and I questioned whether the secrets of lovemaking could be unveiled in a book. Plus, I was positive that going alone would only attract trouble. So, India was out.

However, I had always dreamed of traveling to Peru, sailing over Lake Titicaca, the last gate to remote, unspoiled and serene islands. For Peruvians, Lake Titicaca is sacred. The Incan mythology says that the mighty God Viracocha, rose from the lake and created the world as it is today. So, Lake Titicaca is the birthplace of the Incas, the place where their spirits return to after death. All I could think of was that it wasn't such a bad place to spend your eternity. But, when it comes to my resting place for ever and ever, I could rely on pictures, stories and the taste of others. I needed to check it myself. And that was exactly what I ended up doing. I arrived to Lima, the capital of Peru, in the evening. The first thing that hit me was the horrendous traffic.

"Holiday, *señora*?" the taxi driver asked me.

"Yes," I replied holding the front seat with both hands and taking a deep breath. "The traffic, not good today," I said pointing at the reckless drivers speeding and cutting each other off like on a death race. Suddenly, I wondered how come the greatest Formula One racing drivers were not Peruvians... The only explanation I came up with was that the race had far too many regulations for the free-spirited drivers of Peru.

"Traffic very good today, *señora*. In the morning, *tráfico muy malo*," he responded, laughing at me.

If there is something that makes all of us feel better when things get rough, it's being assured there is still a long way till we hit rock bottom. And so, trying to imagine how much worse or dangerous traffic can get, I started slowly to relax and get into the atmosphere.

The hotel was an old shabby building, with basic rooms and thin walls, some flaking orange paint, and a funny smell of what might have been mold. It did not bother me much. After all, I was in South America and if I was ever to understand and love this part of the world, then it would be for the flavors and its people, not for the comfort or some shiny buildings.

After a fast five minutes tour of my "sumptuous" room, I went back on the streets, the only place where one can feel the pulse of a nation. After a short stroll, I arrived to Plaza de Armas, the core of the city, the birthplace of Lima. It was about ten in the evening on Friday night and the city was fully and truly awake. People of all ages were dancing, embraced, at the sound of *zamponas*, a six feet long panpipe, flutes and *charangos*, their version of the European mandolin. Friday nights were dedicated to love, the love for your partner, for music, for life. And from youngsters to elders, from poor to rich, everyone was out on the streets, dressed colorfully, singing and dancing together.

"A dance, *señora?*"

"Sure. Why not?"

"Una blanca palomita,..."

Then, it was dinnertime. When the stomach speaks, you listen. I followed the smells to narrow, winding streets, packed with people and local restaurants. Finally, I stopped at one serving the most famous food in Peru: *cuy*, otherwise known as fried guinea pig. I ordered it and waited.

"What is this?" I asked the waiter, seeing more bones than meat while the fragrance also left a lot to be desired.

"Guinea pig, *señora*. What else?" he responded politely and humbly.

"What else indeed...bring me the bill, please, and a strong pisco sour cocktail," I said trying to be at least half as nice as he was. The Pisco Sour is Peru's national drink, a cocktail compounded of a shred of hope, a touch of Inca mystery and sublime promises carried on the wings of the Andean condor.

I ended up eating at McDonalds. And then, I finally crashed.

The following day, Puno, the folkloric capital of Peru and the gateway to the islands on Titicaca Lake, was waiting for me.

From there, my first stop was Uros, a group of manmade floating islands. On Uros, there were no stores; everything one needed was at the lake, where the totora reeds grew abundantly. People made everything out of it, including the islands themselves. The tender stems were used in salads or stews; the rest was used as roofing material. In my eyes, totora was a miracle plant, the best example of sustainable living: free, renewable and definitely clean.

The islands were a paradise of a simple, cheap, and happy life. A ninety-five-year-old man still rowing a boat for around eight people was the living proof of that. On his face, I could see everything I was looking for: peace. He belonged to the place the same way the place belonged to him. And this and no other mantra was his secret.

From the manmade islands, I moved on to a God-made island, Amantani. God definitely had more time to work on it, as it was far bigger and far sturdier. However, it also lacked modern amenities, such as electricity or running water.

But to me, the lack of electricity was one of the highlights. As for water, let me put it this way: I was alone. So, it didn't matter too much.

"*Bienvenida a mi casa,*" the local woman, whose family was about to become my family for the next few days, said to me.

Dressed in a black skirt, decorated with red and black embroidered edging, with a poncho and woolen hat and her hands cracked by sun, wind, and work, she gave me a big hug, a strong kiss on both cheeks, took my hand, and showed me the way to her house, the last one on top of the hill.

After a steep climb, tired and a bit nauseous from the smell of gasoline from the boat, my eyes kept searching for the house.

"*Vamos, vamos!*" she kept saying to me. By the look of her hands it must have meant: "Hurry up! Hurry up!"

"I would if I could!" I said back.

She laughed, I laughed, while none of us knew for sure what the other said. Laughing, the international passport to anyone's heart, was working in Peru too.

Finally, we arrived. Her husband, her kids, some of her nieces and nephews too, were all part of the welcoming committee. Each one of them kissed me, hugged me, said a few words, strange to my ears as their faces were to my eyes.

"Wow! So this is love!" I said to myself. "A bit suffocating for my taste. I wonder: Will I sleep alone tonight or with one of the cousins available? Could I choose at least with which one?"

Choosy, choosy, like always! Snooze, snooze, till you lose! the voice in my head replied.

If nothing else, it was definitely more fun having discussions with myself than with anyone else...

The room itself wasn't much, but the bed and the door were quite something. The door was half my height, requiring either a flexible back to bend or a strong head to take the hit. The bed was made out of wood, with no mattress on top, and again, a bit too short for me.

"Some hay and maybe even a roll in the hay would have been somehow more desirable," I thought.

And a strong lover too, I bet! my imagination muse soon added.

"I doubt such a bed allows for more than a friendly hug."

I thought you like it rough, missy?

And before the dialogue took a less decent turn, the lady of the house proclaimed:

"*Hora de la cena!*"

"Sorry?" I asked her, thinking a Spanish-English dictionary would have come in handy.

"Eat, food, *cena*," she continued in a funny accent.

"Food! Why don't you say so? About time," I replied happily.

The kitchen was a small room looking more like a tunnel and lit up by candlelight. We all sat down at a wooden table, crammed into one another, warmed up by the fire from the wood-burning stove, said our prayers to the Gods and to the two mountains on the islands, Paccha Tata and Paccha Mama, Father and Mother Earth, and waited for the feast to arrive.

For vegetarians, it was a paradise, as all the courses were made from potatoes. But the dishes were not boring or tasteless, and I bet any chef in the world would have been quite envious. And although it had no meat, it was much better than the skinny guinea pig I attempted to have a night before or the MacDonald's where I ended up eating.

"Long live the vegetarians!" I said. And I meant every word of it.

I remembered a friend telling me once that out of the five thousand potato varieties worldwide, four thousand grow in Peru and come in countless colors and shapes.

"What do they do with so many potatoes?" I asked him surprised back then. But now, I knew: everything.

During my first night on Amantani, I experienced the most terrifying and beautiful storm ever. In the pitch dark, on my hard-as-stone bed, shivering under the weight of the blankets, I listened to the symphony of thunders. I was a world apart from what I was used to.

However, I was happy and peaceful, just like the old man. I fell asleep thinking to myself, La Vita e Bella: *Benigni was, after all, right.*

When I woke up, the sky was clear, the sun was shining, and hidden under the bed, I found a page from an old travel magazine with pictures of The Great Ocean Road.

All day I thought about it.

Was that a sign? Could it be that simple? Why not? It's not as if only complicated things are worth pursuing, long novels are worth reading and educated people worth listening to. There is a beauty and wholesomeness in simplicity that the eye who have seen it all returns to every time.

Maybe Australia was the answer I was looking for. My heart seemed to agree. And my mind could not find one reason not to. And then, I decided: my next challenge would be emigrating to Australia.

Dora's Journal Notes

- *Looking for reasons, although it might give us something to think about, will never change how we feel.*
- *Everything in life, no matter how good or bad, comes with an expiration date.*
- *Believe in signs, take them for what they are and don't try to interpret them the way you wish the future to be.*

CHAPTER 18

CHALLENGES, OUR OPPORTUNITY TO SHINE

*Challenges are special moments when
We learn to cherish what we had back then,
But more than that they teach you how,
To fight, survive, and never bow!*

"YOU'RE AN OPTIMIST," my friend said to me one day when I told her about how much I still loved my life in Canada.

"I'm a realistic, my dear. Just wearing a different set of glasses than yours."

"Yes, yes, sure," she mocked me. Then, with sorrow in her voice, she continued: "If only you'd have my life..."

"And if only you'd have mine," I said gently, giving her a pat on her back, trying to shake off whatever burdens she was carrying.

"No, thank you."

"You see? Your life is as bad as you think it is, no more and no less."

"How can *you* still love your life in Canada? I cannot understand. After all, it brought you more tears than laughter, more frustration than contentment, and more disappointment than fulfillment. Nothing to love, except for a guy or two."

"True, but it gave me unfettered and sole ownership over my decisions. It gave me freedom. That's not something one can easily forget."

And then, I told her, all the reasons for which I loved Canada: the good, the bad, and yes, the ugly ones too.

"I love Canada for so many reasons. Some I will remember, some I will forget, while others I will never know. Because true love can never be explained and dissected, bit by bit. True love comes and goes as it pleases. You cannot hide its flame, same as you cannot hide its absence.

It taught me how to be a bitch by choice, not by force; to forgive others' actions, but never forget their nature; to be mentally resilient and obstinately follow my dreams; to believe in myself when no one else seems to be overly excited to do the job, to never let go of my cynical humor even when, or especially when, it is pointed out at myself; to take a back seat each time my life spins off into drama, enjoy the show and grab the leading role only when spring is in the air and love is all around.

I learned that, same as wisdom cannot be bestowed upon me while comfortably sitting in the middle of my own bed indulging myself in reading philosophy books or judging others, patience does not mean to sit around, decry your fate, and pray for a change to happen.

In the shadows of being no one, I found true freedom and the courage to spread my wings and make my own mistakes.

It cured one of my deepest fears, the fear of being alone. In solitude, I have learned to love my own company and turn to nature for hope, perspective, and strength.

Simply put, it taught me how to survive the biggest roller coaster ever: life.

Canada is the place where I learned everything I know about myself: my limits, my shortcomings, my strengths. And I did all that by being open to everything people brought my way: disappointment or gratitude, laughter or sorrow, light or darkness.

And this is why," I shouted, "I love Canada! *J'aime le Canada!* My training ground, my dream, my home away from home! But love and belonging are two different things. I owe it to myself to find the place where they meet."

Dora's Journal Notes

- *Stay put and you will remain as such. Jump in and you might get wet. Dive and you might find true happiness.*
- *Don't be afraid of failures. They are the scars of a champion!*
- *Sometimes trying is as important as succeeding.*

CHAPTER 19

WHY J'AIME LE CANADA

Bonjour, bien sûr, comment ça va?
Hello, of course, ne touché me pas.
We might enjoy the same country,
But we'll never be, comment tu sais, amis.

Oh, mais pourquoi, maudits Anglais?
Or better say, you, tête carrée.
We share the skunks, the beavers too,
The touques, the fever et 'ils se foutent.'

And so it goes, day after day,
Pleasantries stand in the way
Quebec serves snails, amour et vin
The rest of it, just pays le prix.

WHEN I LEFT CANADA, Robert gave me three books: one was *How to Be a Canadian*, another one was *Living Abroad in Australia*, and the last one was *Chicken Soup for the Cat and Dog Lover's Soul*.

He told me most Canadians find the first one funny, so I should take it as a test. The second one was just in case I ever get lost, while the third one had to replace an instant happy phone call.

I never had the time or the need to read the last two, but to see how much of a Canadian I became after all, I read the first one.

What follows is a glimpse of Canada through my eyes.

"Hey buddy, wassup?" Robert said picking up his cell.

"Jeez, I haven't heard your voice in years. Not much, not much, dawg," his friend, Paul, answered.

"Cool, cool! Let's hang out tonight at the Timmie's, eh?"

"For sure. See you later, buddy."

And so it goes. Day after day, in Canada, whether you are planning on falling in love, seeing an old friend, or running into your neighbor, it is all easily done in one single place: the local shopping mall. You don't have to search the Internet for local dates or ride your bike far and wide. Shopping malls get the folks together, keeps the cold away, and the wallets light. And the shopping mall Food Courts are the Mecca of any true Canadian. After the usual retail therapy, here comes the big choice: where to eat. The options are countless: Mexican or Greek, Indian or Japanese, Italian or Chinese, Thai or Vietnamese, not that I could ever tell the difference between the last two. The way I always made up my mind was by comparing the queues. Although some would say longer the better, I say shorter, the better. After all, we might be eating Greek, but we are Canadians, time is money, no bailout loans for us.

While walking around Canucks, you should never worry if you look presentable, a bit flashy, or just plain. On the native land of beavers, there is no such thing as fashion and everything goes as long as it's comfy and warm. The wardrobe of each Canadian consists of at least a dozen flannel shirts and another dozen of touques. You can wear them at work, at the mall, in the summer or winter; it really doesn't matter, because all you are saying is: I am Canadian!

Even if you find it difficult to part ways with your pajamas, rest assured, you may still enter any place you'd like. There will be no fingers pointed at you and no gossiping behind your back. Just don't expect any heads to turn around in admiration. But this is something most of us are used to anyway.

The only problem is that even if you look ridiculous or hideous, no one will do you a favor and tell you. People are polite and politically correct to the point of doing you a disservice.

What better example of this than Canadian road manners? If you are at a pedestrian crossing with no traffic lights, the pedestrians will invite you to go, while you will invite them to cross. And the story might take a while. So, if you are in a hurry, just drive, for God's sake.

But, when it comes to blocking the traffic, pedestrians are by far the least of the evils. It seems to be a dark spell over all the highways in Toronto. Once you enter one, you're stuck there for a long time and at rush hour each one of them transforms into a huge parking lot. To use the time efficiently, you should take a driving lesson book and start reading. You might get your chance to practice one day.

Canadians might be polite, sweet, helpful, and all that is good and beautiful in this world, but not when it comes to Americans. Americans were, are, and will probably remain their worst foe, at least the one they openly admit having. For whatever reasons, Canadians and Americans cannot stand each other.

It might be the proximity. Now, if you were stuck for hundreds of years with the same partner, wouldn't you hate him? I know I would.

Or it might be the bad habit of Americans to import the entire Canadian stock of large and extra-large outfits, which forces all the Canadians to stay fit while their friends over the border indulge in "all you can eat."

Whatever it is, it's there to stay, so learn to play neutral.

I loved the Canadian flag, because it's red, simple, and close to nature. However, I found it to be quite deceiving. It shows a maple leaf, which you rarely see considering most of the year is winter anyway. However, what you always see, no matter where you travel in Canada, winter or summer, is Tim Horton's cafés. Everything a dietician will tell you not to eat, you will find at Tim Horton's. It is famous for its sickeningly sweet donuts, filled with sickeningly sweet cream. It serves the worst *double-double* ever known to humans. But it's double. And, as a country that praises itself on having everything big: houses, portions, lakes, falls and whatever else you might imagine, that's good enough. As a true icon, Tim Horton's remains the first morning stop for every true Canadian. It's the hidden daily tax Canadians pay for living in the country of the snowman.

When it comes to bureaucracy, Canadians have their own version, much more polite, but with the same lethal effects. In some countries you may jump any queue by strategically placing an envelope stacked with cash in the hands of the responsible person. In Canada, you are just stuck.

If you have the patience, the best you can do is make a phone call and start listening for an hour or more, shaking with fear that you might get disconnected, to the same beautiful speech: *"We apologize, but currently all the lines are busy. Please wait on the line and someore will be with you shortly."* If you have enough battery power on your phone, you can spend an entire day like that: once in line, it will take ages to get out of it. It is called a paid online hide-and-seek service.

But, with a good range of degrees to choose from, all with minus in front, life in Canada is fun.

If you think it's not cold enough in Toronto, you can always go to Montreal, and if it is still too warm for you, you might try Calgary and so on until you end up in Yellowknife, which reaches temperatures of minus sixty-four Celsius. If it's still not enough, then maybe it's time for you to have some blood tests done.

The national smell found all around Canada is provided by the population of skunks. No one ever complained of the efficiency and prompt service of their scent glands. Their foul odor is strong enough to be carried almost one kilometer by the wind and can be found everywhere, at any time, in unlimited supplies. This traditional all-organic perfume fills the air in spring, autumn, summer, and winter.

Just in case you might ask: no, they do not hibernate.

And one more thing: in Canada, when you don't know what to say, just say thank you. The more the better.

By the way, *thank you* for reading this.

PART THREE

AUSTRALIA, LIVING THE LIFE OF MY DREAMS

"A few years ago we colonised this place with some of our finest felons, thieves, muggers, alcoholics and prostitutes, a strain of depravity which I believe has contributed greatly to this country's amazing vigour and enterprise."
Ian Wooldridge

CHAPTER 20

MELBOURNE: FOOTIE AND SCHIZOPHRENIC WEATHER

Pussy cat, pussy cat where have you been?
I've been to many places far in between
And, out of all, I have to say,
My love for Melbourne goes a long way!

WHY AUSTRALIA? Why not Australia? It was ever farther from my homeland, had poisonous creatures ready to set me free each day of the year, "convicts" roaming freely proud of their heritage, fearsome crocodiles still mourning for their beloved master Steve Irwin, long enough beaches to encircle an entire continent and warm to hot weather all year round. To make it even better, in the Land of Oz, you know with certainty the world will not come to an end today because for you it is already tomorrow. On New Year's you go to bed first and when you wake up somewhere there is still the Old Year. Whether that's good or bad, it depends on how your year has been.

But immigrating to Australia is not an easy thing to do. Whoever tells you differently must be part of the boat people party paddling along for a better life. Usually, they are the ones reaching the shores of Australia faster than anyone else, welcomed by lots of officials, given a free shelter, then used as a bargaining chip at each federal election.

As for me, I was more afraid of swimming than of flying. Traveling the oceans in search of Australia on a small, flimsy boat was not exactly what my heart would desire or my mind advise. Instead, I filled some forms, took a number and said a prayer. And, looking for some reassurance, I bought some books about spiders, sharks, and deadly jellyfish and wait patiently around the fire dreaming of hot sunny days.

After six months, I got the answer: despite having no serious criminal record, I was a wanted woman.

Although, it took Australia six months to invite me onboard, it took me an entire year to say goodbye to Canada.

After all, it's always hard to say goodbye and most of the time it's not because of some profound feelings: it's just the bloody assets.

"What should I take with me and what should I leave behind?" I wondered, looking around my apartment.

Each piece of furniture, each book, each dish had a story. They all reminded me of my humble beginnings, of my struggles, of my fight. "That's how any hoarder begins! Damn it! I'll give you all a free cruise to Australia."

They might not have appreciated it, but I was happy. I could die in peace or live forever blessed.

Out of all the Australian large cities, I picked Melbourne, following the method of exclusion:

"So where shall we land?" I asked myself while sitting impatiently in front of my laptop. "Sydney?"

Nope. Too big, too crowded, not my thing, my friendly inner voice argued.

"Darwin?"

Isn't that the place of cyclones, Japanese bombs, and crocodiles?

"Is it? I thought it was the place where the thermometer does not go down when the sun does and where box jellyfish form a welcoming party committee each time a croc missed you."

It might be both. Not good! Darwin out! Next one.

"Let's see: Canberra?"

Canberra? No way! It's more exciting to be eaten by a croc than die of boredom. Plus, there, you definitely don't perspire. If anything, you expire.

"Perth then?"

Those guys are in a constant state of excitement. Western Australia, the State of Excitement. It must be the mines getting to their head!

"No good. Too much *dolce far niente* never killed anyone, but too much excitement? Hmmm...it just might. Perth is out."

Adelaide?

"I don't know much about it."

Then, maybe you shouldn't. We are not going to Adelaide.

"Cairns? Brisbane?"

Go where the jobs are! Stop fooling around!

"Melbourne?"

Hmmm...not sure. Tell me another one.

"Another one? That's all there is. It's a continent, dear, what do you want? But, if you want to be a Bedouin, that's a different story. Plenty of spots for this one. Right in the center. We have to settle somewhere. So, what's going to be?"

If we have to, we might to. We'll go to Melbourne.

"Amen."

But Melbourne didn't seem to be too excited with my decision. As soon as I got off the plane, it gave me a chilly look without a warning. At eight Celsius in the morning, the city was the least sunny of it all, surpassed only by Canberra. When I landed, I was wearing the same summer dress I did in the forty-five degrees Celsius heat of Dubai, revealing the shape and form of a freezing goddess: me. What better way to warm up than singing?

"*... cold as ice...*"

Foreigners, cold, this song and this artist were saying it all for me.

"You mean *cool* as ice," a guy passing by said, blowing me a kiss.

Just about when I was ready to blow him a kiss back, my inner voice, shouted at me:

Stop singing! It's serious business going on here. You landed in the land of Oz, dream chaser!

"Indeed, I have. I've done it again!"

But there was no point to despair about the weather, as Melbourne is also famous for having four seasons in a day: at night winter sneaks in, in the morning fall takes over, spring shows its shy face around lunch, and summer smiles in all its glory in the afternoon. So, all I had to do was to wait. With such variation two things were clear: I'd never get bored and I'd never be dressed in tune with the season, simply because there was no clear season. My city of choice had a schizophrenic weather meant to drive whoever attempted to make a plan well in advance insane.

But Melbournians are optimistic people who take pride in having a swimming pool in the backyard and try desperately to use it once per year. They must be really scared of hot saunas.

So, let's make one thing clear: Melbourne is not freezing cold, but it's not suffocating hot either. The winter takes its time, and the summer is not in a rush to come. Don't pack just yet! You might be happier where you are!

Dora's Journal Notes

- *In life, few things are worth keeping: travel light.*
- *Too much planning does not guarantee your success. Confidence does.*
- *Be prepared for the worst; let the best surprise you.*
- *Australia, a backwards country always ahead of every other one.*

If seasons take their time, people mimic the seasons. Down under, everything and everyone is a bit slow, not backwards, but just slow. To get the drift, here are two real life examples:

First one, writing an email at work:

"Hi, Janet. I wrote you about three weeks ago in relation to an urgent matter. I have not heard back from you..."

Should I write, "Please respond to your earliest convenience?" I asked myself.

"No, no, no! What will be the point? She does that anyway."

I started again.

"Hi, Janet. Bla bla bla...I look forward to your reply." Whenever that will come.

Second one, waiting for my Aussie lover:

"You know you're late, don't you?"

"No way! Again?" he asked with the face of an angel.

"Yep, that's exactly my point: *again!*"

"Oh, luv, just when I was making an effort."

"Rrright," I said making a mental note to pick the next one anything but Aussie, preferably German-made.

The moral of the stories: in the land of Oz, don't worry, be happy or like they say: no worries, mate! They surely live by those words and you'd better do the same.

Dora's Journal Notes

- *There is a time to run and a time to rest. For Aussies, the first usually happens in the morning, for the second they take all day.*
- *If you are punctual, learn to wait.*

If, after waiting for him for hours, you still have doubts whether he is a true Aussie, wait till he opens his mouth. There is nothing like the Aussie accent. It's unique, impossible to reproduce and even more challenging to understand.

Not convinced yet? Go figure this true example of barbaric butchery of the English language. Then, try turning it into a song: Phew!

I am a fair dinkun aussie,
I luv my mates and footie games,
I've my brekkie early mornin'
And watch my pitches nightie night.
I spend the day missing my missy,
Wait for the Chrissy to hold her tight.
I hate the Poms each time the're picky,
I hate the mozzies and skippies too.
I cook my chooks right on the barbie,
Might throw a prawn, a croc or two.
G'day G'day ya shifty bugger,
It's me your dirty gutsy shagger.
G'day G'day ya ginger luv,
G'day G'day, sis' "ows it goin"?
Shut up you arse or chatter box!
You'd better go and buy some avos,
Or otherwise I'll tell your boss!

However, don't be surprised if they consider others messing up with their native language. Some would rather think you are the one with a Euro trash accent than admitting they are the descendants of Eliza Doolittle.

Their road signs seem also to be a bit "interesting:" "Right turn from left only." Say that again?

Dora's Journal Notes

- *If you speak English, but Australians still have no idea what you are saying, blame it on the accent! Theirs, not yours!*
- *All signs have a purpose, even if only to make you smile or go insane.*

If Toronto sometimes smells like maples and most of the time like skunks, in Melbourne the gum trees are in charge of the fragrance. I loved going for a walk, squashing a leaf in my hand, and letting the eucalyptus oil fill my nostrils.

The sounds are also a bit different. If in Toronto there is no day without hearing the wind blowing, in Melbourne first thing you hear in the morning are the parrots squawking. The parrots are the Australian version of the rooster with one main difference: while the roosters turn quiet after giving you the wake-up call, the parrots are in charge of ensuring you stay awake the whole day. They are louder than your wife, your mother-in-law, and both of them put together.

Christmas is celebrated on the beach, with your hopefully topless girlfriend and her skimpy string bikinis, having a picnic and watching the sunset make the sky burst with colors.

If you love the outdoors, then Melbourne is not a bad place to be. You can go for a bike ride in the mountains or along the ocean shores, you can soak in the mineral outdoor spas, have a glass of wine at the different wineries surrounding the city or simply watch the cockatoos quarrelling with a vocative magpie, a daring kookaburra or a noisy miner. You'll find it easy to understand why Victoria is called the Garden State.

If you were to ask any Melbournians what they love to do most, the answer will be one and one only, and no, it is not lying on the beach. Melbournians love to watch footie, with the only plausible alternative being to play footie. In Ozzy land, footie is a mandatory activity leading to compulsive disorder when missed. Each game has to be watched, then watched again, commented, then commented again. It really doesn't matter with whom. Could be your dad, your cousin, your neighbor, the taxi driver, anyone you meet. The subject is more popular than the weather.

"We're going out tonight, gorgeous! We'll have a blast!" my Aussie boyfriend proudly announced to me.

"Shall I put on my new dress?" I asked.

"A pair of running shoes, black jeans, and a red shirt will be better. It's Anzac Day and the Bombers are playing tonight, luv! How could you forget?" he went on, while his voice became louder.

"How anyone dares to forget!"

"C'mon! We'll have fun! It's the final! Bombers are playing in the final! Do you know what that means? Do you know for how long I've been waiting for this to happen?" he screamed, overly excited.

"If you had to wait that long, clearly they're not that great! OK, OK, we'll go."

And so, we went.

Aussies are a peaceful nation. To give you an example, when the government introduced the famous carbon tax just after announcing another tax, they talked about it for a day or two. Then, everything became a thing of the past.

But, when the footie final is on, everyone goes a bit cuckoo. The streets and the highways are packed.

The time when we went there made no exception.

"We have the best seats. I paid a fortune for them!" he exclaimed.

"Uh, baby, I am so excited!" I made fun of him.

Making a long face, he scolded me:

"One day, you'll get it! And that day, you'll become a true Aussie!"

"Then, I guess I'd better try my best today!"

When the team's theme song started, all fans stood up and sang: "*See the Bombers Fly Up!*"

I had never seen my boyfriend more proud of me than on that day. I was becoming an Aussie.

What I loved the most about the Australians and their footie fetish was that once at the stadium, the supporters of both teams formed quite a happy, passionate choir. You might find yourself chanting for one team, while the guy next to you chants for the other one. If this happens, all you have to do is to scream louder. Other than that, no worries mate, you'll be safe.

After devoting all their energy to the game, no wonder they are exhausted and all the other activities, from sex to work and from work to sex are pursued slowly, but surely.

Beside footie, indulgence in beverages of an alcoholic nature is another Australian favorite way of passing time. Friday's drinks are the highlight of any workplace, a merry time of socializing, vocalizing, promoting and demoting each and every one. And when an Aussie drinks, he drinks: bottle after bottle, the beer seems to go down faster than any other liquid might dare to try.

After five, six to ten bottles and no breaks in between, you might think your boyfriend might be a bit tipsy. Indeed he might be, just as you say, a bit tipsy and ready for the next round.

The women are not much better or much worse, depending on how you look at it. They might prefer some liquor, Irish cream, or other sweet beverages, but that will be all the difference.

Other than that, life in Melbourne can be as boring or as exciting as you fancy.

Just make sure you get used to the English humor, or the lack of it.

CHAPTER 21

A LAWYER'S CHOICE: WHEN PASSION TURNS INTO OBSESSION

Mirror, mirror on the wall
What should I be famous for?
Be a lawyer, here she goes!
What? A lawyer ? No, that's gross.
Be a judge, if you insist!
Better an actor, if you persist.
Be a writer then, you silly!
To die hungry, young, and pretty?
Be a lawyer, as I say: once, twice, sold!
Have it your way!

WHEN IT COMES TO LAW SCHOOL, ever since my parents claimed being a lawyer is the security blanket for a bright future, I've always wondered whether they could be right. My heart was telling me that working as a lawyer is not what would make me happy. But my mind could not find the reasons behind it and always struggled with my decision of aborting the plan and start a different career from scratch. Without some clear proof that it was not for me, turning my back to law seemed to be a bit like *coitus interruptus*, pulling out while you'd still want to be in.

So, when my former Canadian employers who were like a family to me, insisted on paying for my university, I happily enrolled at the second largest university in Australia, to become what is pompously called Juris Doctor or simply said Doctor of Law or even simpler than that, "another" lawyer.

"Luckily, there are only two legal systems in the world, the civil law system and the common law system. Otherwise, who knows how many law degrees I will end up pursuing," I said to Robert over a phone conversation.

"Wrong! You forgot the religious law," he jumped.

"Something tells me the black nun's outfit won't suit me."

"Uh baby! Why not? Are you a sinner?"

"I'm not a saint. Let's leave at that."

"As you wish, Sister Dora."

"Sister *Superior* Dora, *per favore*."

We both laughed. I was happy. Going to law school, again, was another longtime dream. It felt a bit like joining the intelligence club, *la creme de la crème* of society, a safe bet for a good life.

And now, after five years of humiliations, disappointments, and moments of despair, it was finally coming true.

However, after the first few months, I realized that law school was not how I imagined it to be. It wasn't a happy, merry place, where I would rub elbows with wonderful, educated, and smart people.

Most of the teachers were eager to go home sooner rather than later, with no incentive to do what they were doing other than money. Some of my colleagues were still learning how to spell, while others were moving on to the next phase: fighting against depression. Depression seemed to go hand in hand with tons of mandatory reading, assignments and case studies, all done in the solitude of your own house. Whether one was willing to recognize it or not, depression was more like the norm, rather than the exception.

I wasn't too much of a happy camper either. After spending day after day at my desk with boring thick books, cutting all the ties with the outside world, the blues started to practice their courtship rituals on me too. I became exhausted and frustrated.

What law school did to most of us was quite a balancing act: while gaining weight, we were losing friends, while learning abstract concepts we were losing the practicality behind it, and while gaining a title to hang on the wall, we were losing ourselves. This was academically called the selection process.

Some of us, feeling that law was taking over their lives, did themselves justice by getting a life. The rest of us thought they were losers.

Others continued their ascent to peaks of solitude and merit and were labeled as ambitious. I was part of those latter ones.

All of us hoped, once we would finish law school, we would be out of the woods. The end of law school was seen as a finish line which once crossed would lead us to a glamorous, highly paid career, where law, order, and respect prevailed.

This kept all of us going, including myself.

After three long years of compromises and deceptions, I graduated with high distinction. I was a Juris Doctor, a doctor of law, a lawyer in Australia. Another impossible dream came true.

Still, I was neither happier, nor smarter than before. If anything, I was sad and tired. Once again, the only thing I lacked during all the years of law school was enthusiasm and, at the end, the only thing I was not getting out of it was happiness.

For my weekly session of emotional therapy, to take off my chest whatever was crushing my heart, I called Robert.

"What's wrong, sweetie?" he asked, guessing by the sound of my voice that I'd had better days.

"Not much," I replied, aware of how silly it sounded to complain about accomplishing something I wanted so badly to happen.

"You mean, not much is right? C'mon, open up! Women do not snore, burp, sweat, or pass gas. Therefore, they must bitch or they will blow up. Remember?"

"To blow up would not be good, but some bitching on the other hand wouldn't hurt."

"That's my girl. So, what's wrong, eh? Didn't you find the perfect job that lets you stay at home while paying you top bucks?" he laughed.

"I didn't look for it. Maybe I should. Now seriously, I'm not that naïve. But, after graduating with high distinction the second best university in Australia, I did expect to be snapped right away by law firms, offered a position, a decent salary to start with, and a work-life balance. Wouldn't you?"

"And what's happening instead?"

"Every law firm I applied to, and trust me, there were tons of them, is asking me to put my life on hold for another two to three years, get paid less or the same as any sales person at the grocery store, and work twice as much in the hope that one day I will reap the rewards deserved. All for being called a lawyer. Sorry, a junior lawyer. And it's only the tip of the iceberg. Others ask you to work for free, so you can gain experience. It's called a training program."

"Sounds familiar. Remember that job you had at the bakery store, selling cakes? I know what happened after the training period was over: another one started."

"Exactly. It's not fair."

"I remember reading this somewhere: 'If you expect the world to be fair with you because you are fair, you are fooling yourself. That's like expecting a lion not to eat you because you did not eat him.' Anyway, aren't lawyers supposed to be rich?"

"Supposed to be, yes; really be, no. Truth be told, for one lawyer partner who buys a BMW, twenty other junior lawyers are working very hard. At the end of the day most lawyers are neither rich nor famous, but just make an honorable living after working hard for their whole lives."

"That's tough. But you've never been a money chaser, sweetie. And even though it's an issue, is it the only one?"

"There's something else. I thought, once I'll be done with the uni, I'll have a schedule like everyone else: work for eight hours per day, come home, relax, the usual stuff. But no, to make it as a lawyer, I'd have to work ten to twelve hours per day, come rain or shine. Forget about taking more than four weeks per year off and even those in small chunks."

"Sounds like fun!"

"With this kind of schedule, I'll probably never get married, and if I will, I'll get divorced in no time. Those people are working machines. Woody Allen was right, 'Some men are heterosexual, some are bisexual, and some men do not think about sex at all; they become lawyers.'"

"Maybe. Although, technically speaking, even as a lawyer you can think of sex all day long. You just won't get the time to practice it."

"Stop making fun; it's a serious matter."

"Phew! You tell me how serious it is, eh? Sex, no sex, the clock is ticking."

"I remember seeing a French movie once. The guy said, '*ma femme, tous les autres...*'"

"Translation, please?"

"My wife, or all the rest. He could not pick one over the others."

"Or the choice was too obvious."

"The idea is the same with law: law or sex, sex or law. It's almost like you'd have to choose."

"Choose? I know a lot of women who live just fine without being lawyers. But without sex? Phew! They all go nuts! No offense."

"None taken."

"It sounds like as a lawyer your work days will be too long for just one life. On the other hand, I dare to say, you know from your own life there are people out there working night and day for even a lesser amount of money than a lawyer makes and with no prospects whatsoever. Also, divorce is not a trademark for lawyers. It's such a widespread phenomenon then when it's happening to you, it's difficult to come up with a different set of reasons other than your friends have. So, I might not throw this last aspect into the equation."

"It's just that working long hours, putting up with all those clients who blame you instead of trying to change the system, hoping someday it will all be worth it, is not my dream."

"But it's what being a lawyer means. And you wanted to be a lawyer. *Quod erat demonstrandum.* It's your dream. So, maybe next time, before wantin' something to happen, you should make sure you know what it involves."

"Stereotyping and assuming: one step further towards ignorance. I guess this is what I've done."

"Yep. The highest form of ignorance is having firm convictions about something you only have ideas of."

"True. All those years, I ignored everything around me and focused all my efforts into only one direction: law school. There was no life beyond law and I didn't want to achieve anything else other than becoming a lawyer."

"It was a risky investment. And like every other risky investment, it could yield higher profits or drive you straight into the ground. You placed all the bets on one card knowing you're a poor loser, sweetie."

"And this was wrong."

"Yes, it was. But you had to do it. There was no other way for you to find out. You wouldn't have listened to anyone. The universe tried to stop you so many times; it gave you so many signs. But, you're as stubborn as you're beautiful. Maybe next time you should try to be more generous with your passion, and sprinkle some into all areas of your life."

"You're right. Each time I was close of working as a lawyer, something intervened and my life changed again, always for the better. Each refusal I got, it was a blessing in disguise. But how could I not see it? I wasted so much time, money, and effort."

"Go easy on yourself. We all see what we wanna see. Plus, when the reality hits, the reasons behind it are less important. What will you do next is all that matters. Maybe it's time for you to finally accept who you are, what you truly want out of life and go for it."

"Maybe...I don't know. I'm confused. I feel lost, unappreciated, cheated, and all the other 'goodies' put together."

"What about your ego?"

"He's the only winner. He got what he wanted. My ego is fed, but I'm fed up with it."

"That's a positive start."

"I haven't told you yet. Not quite everyone turned a blind eye to my legal knowledge, outstanding results and two highly revered diplomas. I was accepted into a prestigious program in private international law in The Hague. I might just go for it."

"Wow! Somebody does not give up, eh?"

"It's so hard to give up on something you hold onto for so long. In a way it becomes part of you."

"So does a gangrene."

"I know, but it's hard to know when to stop, when to give up, when the fight is over. You get accustomed to suffering more than you get accustomed to jump."

"Is that how a winner talks?"

"No, I guess not. I guess a winner will always choose to jump than to die on a sinking ship. Maybe I'm not a winner after all."

"Or maybe you just don't know it yet. But you will, sooner or later. Sooner being the preferred choice. Just go with the flow and watch for the signs. You've always done it this way."

"How can I ever thank you for always being there for me?"

"Having confidence in yourself will be a good start. Now, go! The dreams are callin'..."

"Have a good night or whatever is left of it. I am sorry for keeping you so long on the phone," I said realizing in Canada it must have been past midnight.

"Don't worry. I'll get enough sleep when I'll be six feet under. It was time well wasted."

"Love you."

"Love you too, sweetie."

Dora's Journal Notes

- *Life is the toughest teacher: we cannot skip a lesson and still pass.*
- *Pouring all your passion into only one area of your life is a bit like playing the Russian roulette. If you cannot stand to lose everything, then it is wrong for you to play it.*
- *Same as marriage does not make one in love or riches does not make one happy, school does not make one smarter.*
- *Nobody likes lawyers, but everyone feels they should be the judge.*

CHAPTER 22

LUST AND OTHER DEMONS

Falling in love is never kind
Lust is lost and you are blind.
That is why, when it comes to men,
Hump them, bang them, scream hooray!

TO TAKE MY MIND OFF LAW but not quite, in my last trimester of law school, God sent me another provocation: a tense, sexy lawyer, all alone, who needed to be discovered, comforted, and all in between.

We met during a mediation session.

"Hi, my name is Dora. I'll be your mediator today."

"Our mediator?" he asked, a bit surprised.

"Yes, do you have anything against it?"

"No, not really, just that... Aren't you a bit too young for this?"

"For this? No. For you? I might be," I answered, a bit annoyed by his remarks.

Nevertheless, there was something intriguing about him. I could sense he was the dangerous kind, one of those guys who charms you, has you, and lets you cry in the rain. And then I knew: the challenge was about to begin.

The following day, I got his email:

"Dear Miss Dora, I like you. Let's go for a coffee together. Tomorrow will be great if it suits you. Kind regards..."

I replied:

"Firstly, please do not call me Miss. You make me sound either important or as one of Dickens' characters. I am lucky enough to be neither. Dora or even 'mate' sounds way better. Secondly, I don't drink coffee, I drink tea. Thirdly, let's go for a walk and then to a spa together. Lastly, please keep those 'kind regards' of yours for more solemn occasions. See you, stranger! Dora."

That's when my new romance started: challenging, exciting, eye-opening, and most of all, passionate. It took me deep into the forbidden gardens of pleasures, blindfolded and guided only by my insatiable desire for lust. I did what I never dared to do before: I reached for sexual fulfillment. I did not hold back emotions or words, I did not put a stop to my fantasies, and I did not let fear or shame to spoil my fun.

Why him? I didn't know back then and I don't care to find out now.

All I know is I found how pure lust feels, what a multiple orgasm is, and that in all of us lies a dormant rabbit wanting to mate all day, all night, and everywhere it can. Although much better than finding out I am a koala, wanting nothing else than to sleep all day and all night, it was not less worrying.

Before going into the nitty-gritty details, let me start by saying: Before, I never let myself swayed by the physical beauty of a man.

I always considered it a matter of pride to be with an intelligent man rather than just a handsome one. As for those rare cases when those two qualities meet, I thought it's such a rare event that you must be born in the lucky year, lucky day, lucky hour, to happen to you. And even then, it would be selfish and silly to expect they will belong only to you forever and ever, amen. But, sharing a man was never my forte.

In the end, I made myself believe that as they say, the beauty is in the eye of the beholder and any decent man will be a much better match than any *homme fatale*.

But, now and then, you start questioning your beliefs and you start aiming for the moon in broad daylight.

And this is what was happening to me now.

He picked me up from my house in his casual shorts, un-ironed T-shirt, and flip flops, proudly driving his beauty down my driveway.

"A BMW? Ha! You know what it means?"

"No," he said.

"Bring Me Women, silly."

"Just a coincidence. I assure you it is not the case," he smiled.

"And the plate number, 'AHA69,' a coincidence as well, I assume."

"Coincidence indeed," he replied, this time quite amused. "Get in! We have a long day ahead!"

And long it was. First, we got lost and we could not find the place where we were supposed to go for a walk. Then, we finally got there and, when after two hours of walking we wanted to go to the spa, we could not find our way back to the car. In the end, after another five hours of walking around in circles, we found the car, but we could not find the spa. Once down at the spa, he could not find his towel, but thank heavens he found his bathers. The beginning was promising.

Just when I was about to relax, he tried to kiss me. I refused: Once, twice, and then my whole world changed. This time, we were truly and fully lost.

There was something about him that was setting me free, making me go for it without shame. It might have been his intoxicating smell, his handsome muscular figure, his deep green eyes, his grave voice, his childish spoiled lack of manners, his huge best friend he was so proud of, or maybe, just maybe he was the right guy at the right moment with the right me.

After months of teasing, the real thing finally happened:

"*Do you wanna touch...* ?"

"What are you singing there? Is it Joan Jett, the Blackhearts?" I asked him wondering what was going through his head.

"Yes, it's her. And I'm not *only* singing. I am speaking my mind," he said, looking straight into my eyes, provocative, alluring, promising many days of pleasure and even more of pain.

"I see..."

I could hear my heart, but I could not feel my knees, I could see him, but I could smell him even better. He fascinated me from the first moment I've seen him. There was no way I could deny this simple truth. And, except for an overwhelming fear of losing control of my heart, I had no reasons to.

Be yourself, everyone says when we're in trouble. But how can we be ourselves if we don't know what it means? And how could we, if we never let ourselves go? If we're always scared of slipping, scared of having it all. But one day, something happens. And in that day we become more fearful of silence than of noise, more frightened of comfort than of adventure, more worried of making no mistakes than of dealing with them. That day, we are born again, that day we become ourselves.

And that was my day. All I wanted to do was to give myself to him, wholly and truly, to let whatever was coming over me fill my mind, wake up my senses and question everything I thought I knew about relationships. That day I allowed myself to be swayed by lust.

"So, what's the answer?" he went on, pushing my back against the wall.

"Yeah, I want to touch you: here, there, everywhere!" I responded and rolled into bed with him.

A few hours later, cuddling in his arms, I was still unsure about what I wanted to do first: catch my breath or do it all over again. Making love to him was a dream, this time an unplanned one, but no less amazing. Despite not being a virgin, I felt like I was; despite not being a sinner, I felt I would die to become one. Now that the game was on, I did not want it to stop and I doubted I would ever want.

"Uh, that was something!" I said softly. My body was exhausted, but I was totally relaxed. I was happy and excited and part of me was already picturing the day when we will walk down the aisle.

"Take it easy, it's just sex. Pretty good one though! And the night is still young," he replied, jumping out of the bed and turning on the TV on the footie channel.

I always found all the words equally beautiful. There is a moment, a place and a person for all of them. There is a place, a moment, a person for sex, for shag, for making love, for mating, for copulating, for rolling in the hay, for humping and for whatever other is out there.

But now, it was not the moment, not the place for *sex*. And I was not the right person for it.

His words sounded like an alarm bell and I was fully awake. The picture was changing. I seriously needed to reflect on the assumptions I carried about the whole thing. After all, he was the kind of guy who charms you, has you, and lets you cry in the rain. What was I thinking? Probably what lots of women are thinking: I will be *the one* who will change him. Silly, I was not *the one*, I was just *another one*. And it was time for me to face it: take it or leave it, but don't ask for more. "Just sex, huh? OK. Have it your way, stallion," I told him, still hoping he'd say something that would make those harsh words go away, hoping he wanted all of me for ever and ever, same as I wanted him. But, he didn't. He remained silent. And he broke my heart.

Ever since that day, he went by the name of Stallion, while I was known as his Trouble.

I could write for hours about our trips, the cafes we went to, the parties we joined, his favorite dish that always happened to be mine too, his annoying habit of always being late, and so on. But, ever since that day, none of them really mattered.

That day, I decided that I didn't want to know anything about his life. No good could have come out of it. He would take more and more of me, while I would remain with the same thing: great sex with no strings attached. He was too much into himself to let even a tiny bit of him go to another. He enjoyed a fling, a good shag, a glass of wine and a chat, and he was the perfect guy for all these. He was a lover boy and the rest came with the territory.

Now, that I was certain of it, all I wanted was to let him have me, over and over again. I wanted to satisfy my thirst for lust, to allow myself to dissolve in sensual pleasure, to adore his body and let it become the master of mine.

Like the sun, my desire nurtured and burned my heart while my days with him were passing slowly, surely, and definitely not purely.

Each time, he was taking me to new virgin territories of pure pleasure, making me feel like a starlet who finally found her stallion: amazing.

There was never enough, there was only more.

He was pushing himself inside me, looking into my eyes, going faster and faster until I was moaning with pleasure, making me come over and over again until I did not have the energy to move, to scream, or to beg for more.

"The neighbors definitely heard us. I think they hate us by now," I said after one of those sex therapy sessions that felt like the whole apartment might just crumble before us realizing anything else, other than what we were doing.

"You think so?" he joked, imitating my voice during climax. Oh, he was cute! But not as loud as I was.

"Stop it!" I said, blushing.

"Stop it? That's new! You mean, continue?" he teased me. "You want it! You always want it! You'll kill me before saying you don't want it anymore!" He bit my lips gently, the pain slowly increasing. He knew I loved it, just a bit of pain, enough to keep me in the moment.

"I am exhausted! I am all sweaty," I complained.

"You, exhausted? That's new again! What is sweat when compared with pleasure, gorgeous?"

"I guess we'll find out soon enough, Stallion," I replied, jumping on top of him, the signal his break was over.

And so it was. Day after day. Night after night.

Sex with him was my freedom statement, my detox session, my body and mind exercise. It was powerful, but beautiful, overwhelming but enlightening, scary but liberating.

I was dancing close to a fire: I could feel its warmth, its charm, and its dangerous side. I liked to feel my wings starting to burn just so I could move farther before it would blind me forever.

Each time, my voice screaming out loud without holding back my emotions and his voice following mine shortly after, sounded like a beautiful song without any melody or definite rhythm. Together our fantasies were becoming reality, one by one. I could tantalize him with a private striptease session at his office after hours, when he was looking so tense, tired, and so sexy in his lawyer outfit. I could take off my shirt and bounce my tits after a long, strenuous hike without a worry in the world. Or, we could rush home and go straight for a good one, leaning against the entrance door before turning on the lights, taking off our shoes, or taking a shower.

I loved to watch our bodies performing acts I didn't know they knew. It was like they had a mind of their own in which I had nothing to say. I loved to see our hearts coming together for a second only, then going separate ways, dissolved in the power of the mind.

There was no shame, no fear of embarrassment, no anxiety, no place better than another, no rose petals scenario, no well-rehearsed right words spoken softly. I was not concerned with pleasing him and he was not concerned with pleasing me and this made it all happen.

Nothing was ordinary or too much, nothing was appropriate, courteous, or predictable. It was as it should always be. And we both loved it this way.

With him, I was myself: dancing without music, singing without a reason, saying the words I wanted to say, living my deepest sexual fantasies just to wake up full of desire and loved slowly before even saying good morning.

With him, I was the sexually-obsessed one, the princess of madness and change, the one who loved all men, made love with all, and still remained a virgin. I was the tree of all that is feminine and all that is not. I was the traveler who left home just to find him.

I was finding my own balance in the pure bliss of temporarily loving a man until exhaustion. But I knew that, for each chest we lean on, each lips we touch, each eyes we cherish, there is a price to pay. And I knew his price. I knew one day he would vanish, disappear, the same way he came: unexpected. I just hoped that time would come late, if ever.

In that last day, when pleasure would turn into poison, all I wanted was for us to make love again with the same passion the prey fights against the predator, knowing it's her final act. At the end, before him opening the bra of another and me unbuttoning the shirt of another, I wanted to feel him inside me one more time, let ecstasy rule my world and then I could let it all go.

That last time came at Uluru.

Dora's Journal Notes

- *Feel the **Lust**, get **Lost** in it, hope it will **Last**.*
- *If sometimes less is more, there are times when more is better.*
- *Lust alone cannot sustain a relationship, but you need it in order to start one.*
- *When love pales, break free before hates sneaks in.*

CHAPTER 23

ULURU: A TRIP TO AUSTRALIA'S RED CENTER

When in Trouble scream and shout,
Don't be shy, let it all out,
But if Trouble screams at you,
Run as far as Uluru!

IF YOU NEVER DREAMT of traveling to Australia, then you're not dreaming properly. But, if you did, probably the first place that comes to mind is Uluru.

I wanted to see Uluru though the eyes of an Aussie, my Aussie, him.

We arrived in Alice Springs in May, late at night, a few days before his birthday. We were not impressed.

"Wow! That's a small city, more like a village really."

"Yes, it's going to be a bit difficult to get lost in it, even for us," I joked, thinking of our long history of incidents.

"Want to bet?"

"No, I don't!"

"Too late! I cannot seem to find the hotel. In case you didn't notice, we've been driving in circles for quite a while."

"Were we?" I said, surprised.

He looked at me, I looked at him, and we both started to laugh. Then, he assured me:

"It's just us, baby. We'll make it till dawn."

In the morning, things got a little bit clearer and we soon realized that in Alice Springs all the streets lead to a big main one where you can find everything and everyone: the grocery store, the police, the hospital, the post office, the lawyers, the homeless, the tourists, the residents. Some will say it's quite boring. But, we found it quite charming in all its simplicity. And I believe another two thousand Americans who choose to call Alice Springs their home will agree with me.

After having our breakfast in a barred restaurant preventing the Aboriginals from breaking in during the night, we left for Kings Canyon.

With only one main dirt road and desert all around us, this time we were on the right track. Hopefully...

All the way, it was just us, the red dirt, and the radio. No worries in the world, no clouds in the sky, and no cars passing by for miles and miles.

When we arrived at the Kings Canyon Resort, it was pouring rain. The locals were happy, saying they didn't see that much rain in years. We spent the first two days inside waiting for the rain to stop. On the third day we awoke to beautiful sunshine streaming in through our French bedroom window.

"Happy Birthday, Stallion!" I said kissing him softly. "Congratulations, you made it another year! So, how do you feel? Wiser, older, or just both?"

"None. Just a bit exhausted after two days with you in bed!"

"Lucky, ungrateful bastard!"

"Just speaking the truth..."

"Let this be your only complaint for the next year! But for now, let's make this day one to remember! We'll go for a hike at the Rim Walk at Kings Canyon, watch the sunset over the red cliffs, have a lovely dinner, and as for the rest, let's just wait and see how good of a boy you are! So, get ready! We are leaving in ten minutes. And don't forget: slip, slop, slap!"

"Yes, sir! Sorry, I meant Madam! Miss Dora! Baby! My baby!" he exclaimed all naked, bowing down before me like a clown.

"You may raise now, and please get dressed. Your lady is waiting."

Despite starting with a heart attack-inducing hill, the walk was one of the most beautiful trails I've ever been to: sandstone domes, rocks dropping sharply three hundred meters, crevices and bizarre animal-shaped mounds, were all a sight to behold. It was hard to decide whether to stop in awe or to continue exploring, carried by the magic of the place.

Then, hidden in the middle of huge sandstone cliff, we found the Garden of Eden, a spectacular oasis where the natural spring waterhole was surrounded by greenery no one would expect to see amongst such a rocky and harsh landscape. We were blown away by the beauty of it all.

"Let's jump in!" he said enthusiastically.

"The water is freezing. I'm not jumping!"

"I'll warm you up. You know I always do. I'm a hottie!"

And before I could respond, he took off first his T-shirt, then his shorts, his boxers, and naked in all his splendor, jumped into the water, screaming:

"Come on, gorgeous! Splish-splash, splish-splash!"

"Crazy guy!" I jumped screaming.

Completely naked in the deep blue cold water, surrounded by hundreds of meters high red cliffs, ferns, and palm trees, I forgot who I was and time stood still. For a moment, I was Eve embraced by Adam in the Garden of Eden. It was a surreal feeling.

On our way back, as darkness fell, we stopped and looked at the sky. From time to time, you could see shooting stars, more than anyone could ever count. In the pitch dark, freezing cold temperatures, in complete silence, we made love. And for the second time that day, the time stood still.

Back at the resort, we went for dinner at the local restaurant.

"So, what are you going to have for dinner on your birthday?"

"A kangaroo steak or even two after such a day!"

But, before we could decide, the playing band's singer shouted, pointing at us:

"This song is dedicated to the lovely couple over there."

Then, she asked him:

"Is she your wife?"

"Yes, we're on our honeymoon," he responded, laughing.

"I know someone will get lucky tonight," she went.

Everyone laughed looking at us with even more interest than before.

"Your wife is very beautiful. You'd better take good care of her, before someone else does."

And then, the song came: *Give me a home among the gum trees...*

He was right; it felt like a perfect day of a perfect, unreal honeymoon. Unfortunately or who knows, maybe fortunately, it was not. Everyone sang happy birthday to him and there, in the middle of nowhere, we danced, surrounded by a big happy group of French tourists singing along.

Slowly but surely the beauty of the outback Australia and its spirit was catching up with both of us.

"You're drunk," I said to him back in the room.

"Love drunk, you mean. I want you! I want you! I want you! Do you hear me? Tonight, I want to fall asleep inside you."

"The last bit...can we change it into something a little bit more exciting than falling asleep?"

"How many times did I fall asleep *inside* you baby? Never! I cannot even fall asleep *beside* you! You are a devious, mischievous, sexy creature who likes to squeeze every drop of energy I have in the most pleasant way a man can dream of! And I want you so badly!"

"I'm all yours, Stallion!"

"Do you think we'll always be together?" I asked him just before drifting off to slumberland.

"Who cares? Maybe yes, maybe not."

"How I love your sincerity!" I said, feeling suddenly mournful. Why he couldn't say *I love you and nothing will change that. We'll always be together?* What was so damn hard? Why we couldn't end a dream day in a dreamy manner? My heart sank.

"And how I love your serious tone, little planner!" he went on, almost asleep.

The next day we drove to Uluru, the famous Australian icon. More majestic than one could imagine, more beautiful than all the postcards in the world show it, Uluru was spectacular. Seeing Uluru was a long time wish coming true.

Around the base, we could see the sacred caves where the Aboriginals lived and prepared for the ceremonies. Unfortunately, the walk was along the bush, in full sun, and we were entirely at the mercy of millions of flies.

"That's why you're flies, to fly, not to sit on top of my nose!" I screamed, annoyed.

"The flies like you, baby!"

"You like me too and you're not always on top of me."

"Now tell me that's not a shame!"

"Ha! Plus, I'm afraid they like everyone! If we stopped for a few minutes, we'd be covered in them in no time!"

"Welcome to Central Australia. Human population: sixty thousand; fly population: a few billions, and still counting."

We watched the sun going down on this magnificent three hundred and forty eight meters rock, higher than Tour Eiffel, on one of the watching platforms, with a beer in our hands. It was spectacular: the reddish-brown monolith surrounded by red dirt changed its color from flaming red to orange and slowly into purple. We felt blessed to be there.

"All my life I chased time just so I could see places like this one. All unique in their own right, all having a story of their own, all beautiful and waiting to be discovered layer by layer. Some places stroked me with their beauty, like Queensland. Others, like Uluru, challenged my mind, my senses and waited to be found, understood and ultimately loved."

"Tomorrow, when we'll go back home, we'll miss it," he said and I could sense both fear and regret in his voice.

"Yes, I'll definitely miss this land where the dingoes roam freely and the wild brumbies reinvent the notion of freedom."

"I'll miss the red sticking dirt, the multi-colored, layered mineral ochre pits, the Gouldian Finch hidden in the bush, and gum trees."

"There is so much you can hear in the silence. So much you can see in the dust. There is so much more than meets the eyes in this arid desert."

"We'll come back."

"Perhaps," I said softly.

My short trip to Central Australia became a reminder that true beauty can be found even in the most arid and unwelcoming places and that attaining true happiness is entirely within our power no matter if we are laying on a beach in Hawaii, in an expensive resort in Tahiti, or just hiking the Kings Canyon and having a simple dinner at a local pub.

I broke up with him at Uluru. Back then, he did not know that. Why should he have known? I did not want to give a tragic endnote to a beautiful relationship. Our story together ended as it should have: at midnight, passionately making love in a huge indoor spa, intoxicated with love, champagne and lust and surrounded by red rocks. Uluru was my goodbye gift for him.

Dora's Journal Notes

- *The best things in life are free, they happen when you least expect them to, and can be found in the most unusual places.*
- *Let men know you from neck down and you will be safe from the neck up.*
- *Without passion, making love is a simple exercise to maintain possession of an already dead relationship.*

CHAPTER 24

BECAUSE IT HAS TO FEEL RIGHT

Each story has to have an end,
It's useless otherwise to pretend.
If it is merry or a bit sad,
It's pointless if the story is bad.
Enjoy the tale, make it matter,
And if it's love, it's all the better!

"ARE YOU OUT OF YOUR MIND? What's wrong with you, girl? Why do you want to leave him? He's a stallion, for God's sake!" Robert asked me half serious, half joking.

"Something doesn't feel right."

"Here she goes again: choosy, choosy..."

"You can call me choosy, spoiled, fussy, picky, or whatever. And you can be right. But this won't change how I feel. And we have to go with what we feel, not with what we wish we would feel or even worse with what others think we should feel."

"Can you imagine? As we speak, millions of people are having sex, thousands of them kiss and hundreds of them cuddle. And what am I doing? I am talkin'. Sure, that's nice too. But only 'cause I'm talkin' to you. It's not only that something doesn't feel right, something is definitely not right."

"You'll get your turn."

"If each time I'll have to wait that long, I'd better learn how to cut the line. But when I'll get it, trust me, I won't complain *something doesn't feel right,* like you do now, missy," he said, laughing.

"Sure, make fun of me now."

"He went to great lengths to charm you," he teased me.

"Great lengths indeed," I responded cracking a smile.

"You didn't lose your sense of humor, sweetie. Now, what do you mean it doesn't feel right? You gotta have some logical reasons."

"No, I don't have to have logical reasons. You don't stay in a relationship because logically speaking it makes perfect sense. You stay because you *feel* it's the right thing for you. The relationships based only on logical reasons are the first ones to turn sour. Why is that?"

"Because she's crazy. Women are all a bit crazy."

"Maybe...but, most likely, it's because something is missing and has been missing ever since the beginning. But, they denied it. They chose to listen to those logical reasons. It really doesn't matter what it is. It could be anything."

"I bet this is how she thinks. After a while, all women look for trouble."

"Sure... When I get married I want to get married for life. And to have a chance for this to happen, I want to give it my best shot."

"And how do you propose to do that?"

"For a start, I'm not going to walk around with a qualities check list he must have and start ticking them off one by one. Handsome? OK. Good family? OK. Stable? OK. And, after adding and subtracting, say the magic word: sold. If I were to do that, Stallion would be my guy."

"A woman without a hidden agenda? Wow! That's somethin'!"

"Thanks for the compliment, Robert," I said, feeling mocked.

"Now, don't flip out. You're part of the nice but still crazy ones, the ones with no hidden agendas, but with no logical reasons either. Go on, you have my full attention."

"His bank account, his mood and even *his pride and glory* could go up and down."

"I'm afraid if you leave him, you might be the one going up and down, thinkin' of him going up and down on you. But if you stay...Oh, if you stay, don't worry, his challenge with you will always be, the same that it's now: to go down, not up."

"Envious?"

"You bet. Me and another few million men on the planet. But please, continue."

"His eyes will get wrinkles and I'll get both wrinkles and cellulite. What's going to happen then?"

"A detox clinic and some Botox?"

"You miss the point. What I'm trying to say is that all those logical reasons for which you stay with someone now, might change over time. On the other hand, if it feels right, you'll always be there, next to him, no matter the tide."

"That's noble of you!"

"I've been with rich, well-off, and just regular guys, handsome or just plain, some were more my friends than my lovers, like you are, others were more my lovers than my friends, like Stallion is."

"And none of them felt right."

"Exactly. You don't know the winning combination. But the only way to find it out is to trust your gut feeling and go with the flow; have patience, confidence rather than ticking off lists; more than anything else, have the courage to keep looking."

"Don't you forget something? What if time is running out? You're getting older, you might wanna settle down, make it easy on yourself."

"That's like asking someone if they want to have a long, but monotonous life or a short, spicy one that feels right for them. I don't think there is a universal answer to this question. But whatever answer we decide to give, we have to feel comfortable with it. This should be our only concern."

"And you gave your own answer. You want someone who just feels right, even if this will mean you'll look for him your whole life, eh?"

"Yes. That's right. Remember? I'm a dream chaser. I'm not a comfort lover. And I know, like with any other dream, if we don't give up too soon or too fast, it will come true. When it will feel right, I will know I found my man. The rest will be just details."

"Wow! Even his best huge 'friend' will be just a minor detail?"

"Even he. True love beside lust should also bring me confidence in the future, peace of mind, and a sense of belonging. That 'one and only' will not only make me feel dizzy with desire, but will also be someone I can rely on, trust, someone who will want to be part of the team called 'Us.' Stallion doesn't want that."

"So size doesn't matter after all. Yay! That's a relief!"

"No, it doesn't. But, ask me again after a few months of not being with him. I might reconsider."

We laughed.

"A stallion is always in high demand, sweetie. He'll be snapped from the market as soon as you set him free. Don't tell me I didn't warn you."

"It's a free market…"

"And too damn volatile…" Robert added.

Dora's Journal Notes

- *The more you please others, the less you will please yourself.*
- *If you can always see when a man wants sex, you can always hear when a woman doesn't.*
- *Isn't it ironic that with a stallion you cannot have a stable relationship?*

CHAPTER 25

BALI: THE LAND OF A THOUSAND TEMPLES AND A MILLION DISASTERS

When the world is not OK,
Take a friend and run away.
Don't look back, forget it all,
Life is beautiful overall!

A BEAUTIFUL QUOTE by the German writer, Hans Magnus Enzensberger, says:
"It all depends on the distance. If you get the correct perspective and the best possible stance then nothing can go wrong." And right he is!

It's fascinating what a distorted image you get, how many things you just don't see if you stay too close to something or someone.

Whenever I'm in doubt, time and distance are my best friends. They help me to detach and see things and people for what they truly are. Once this happens, I can prepare myself and step quietly and contently towards a new phase, whatever it might entail.

To pull myself together, I ran away from Stallion to Bali. Jessica, a friend of mine, thought it will be a good idea to join me in those times of pain and sorrow and came with me.

"Is it raining outside?" Jessica asked as soon as we got off the plane.

"It must be. But look inside the airport. It rains here too," I said, pointing out to the large holes in the ceiling, which were leaving in everything that belonged out: the fresh breeze, the rain and the annoying flies.

"Those Balinese people must really love nature..."

Then, to get the entry stamp, together with a large number of tourists, we waited patiently, on a single long line at the end of which an officer was slowly moving taking his time.

"This guy is slow. What is he? A sloth or something? Why does it take him ages to put a stamp on a passport?" I asked her, a bit tired and cranky.

"Relax! You're on holiday."

"Am I on holiday? I think he's on holiday. Now and for the rest of his life. Amen."

After the precious stamp was carefully applied, we went to pick up our luggage. Used to the Balinese customs, we waited patiently again around the carousel. Only this time, our wait was in vain. They were lost and after a few hours of bickering back and forth, we had to face the truth. All we could do was just hope they were not left to rot in the rain.

Frustrated, we jumped into a taxi, eager to get to the hotel, unwind, and have a nap. The name of the taxi company was *Smooth* Operator, but like everything else in Indonesia, the name was deceiving too.

"Wow! This ride is a bit bumpy!"

"More like a roller coaster, really," I replied, trying not to bite my lips or tongue while talking.

"Why do people keep honking? Don't they have some other kind of music they would like to listen to? Something more soothing, perhaps."

"Jessica, relax! Someone told me we're on holiday."

"And that someone was right. We are on holiday, just not the right one. Welcome to Bali, the land of a thousand temples and a million disasters. I need a good Balinese massage, a strong cocktail and above all, I need to fall in love!" she exclaimed, trying to stay positive.

"We came here to fall out of love! Remember?"

"Speak for yourself. You had your share with that stallion of yours."

"I figured it will be nice to have dirty memories before I settle down."

"Dirty memories before you settle down? Ha! What for? To haunt you? No, thanks. If I find one, I'll tie him to a chair and still marry him."

"Don't blame you," I said, wishing Stallion was there with me.

"Someone is sorry already! It's a fine line between pleasure and pain..."

"Then, why do we cross it, I wonder?" I replied, this time whining, ready to burst into tears.

"What do you mean why? So we can be with the one and only! You'll be just fine!" Jessica assured me, sympathetic.

"Am I not always..."

"You just need a shag. The withdrawal symptoms are kicking in," Jessica said laughing.

"A shag? No, thanks. A shag won't make me feel any different."

"Pardonnez moi, I should've said a *good* shag for a good lady."

"Someone talks from experience," I added.

"And is not afraid to admit it."

"Do you think he misses me?"

"Misses you? He would be crazy if he wouldn't."

"Maybe he is. Aren't we all a bit crazy? After all, I was crazy too, crazy in love."

After we settled in, we had a nap and got acquainted with our gecko roommates. Then, we went out to rent a motorbike.

Surprisingly enough, the guy at the rental office didn't ask us for any kind of license. He just said:

"In Bali, when you drive, you can be drunk or sober or a bit of both. It won't matter much. But what I would advise you though, is to say your prayer, as riding a motorbike here can be a dangerous fun."

We didn't get right away what he meant by that. But, as soon as we were out in traffic, his words sounded in our ears: so wise and so true.

With no traffic rules or none enforced, the cars were stuck in traffic while the motorcycles were in a semi-illegal continuous passing maneuver.

If at the start we were a bit shy, and by that I mean respectful of traffic laws, it took less than three other motorcycles passing us on both sides at the same time, to get the drift and start doing the same to others.

"Freedom!" Jessica screamed, excited.

"Anarchy!" I screamed back, scared.

"Same thing, really! Hold on tight! Here we go!" she said, twisting the throttle to the limit.

"Oh my God! Where have I come?" I wondered, all in panic.

"This is heaven! We will die happy here!"

"Die?"

Before I could say more, Jessica, blinded by dust or maybe just joy, went right through a huge mud puddle, changing in a second the colors of our clothes into only one: dark black. Were we not in heaven, indeed?

I'll never cease to be amazed by how much our vision of a place can differ from the reality.

Before getting to Bali, I pictured it as a terrestrial piece of celestial heaven: palm trees, long white beaches, cheap cocktails, delicious safe food, beautiful rice paddies, good massages, all giving me the peace and relaxation I needed.

Now, I was swearing I would never go back: not for anyone and particularly not if I am looking for Mr. Peace and Mrs. Quiet or both.

Despite her optimism and love for dangerous driving, after just a few days, even Jessica was sick and tired of it all.

"That's it! I had enough! We're leaving today! We're going to Ubud!"

"Ubud, the Mecca of the artists or lost souls looking to heal. Why not? Ubud might be just the right place for us," I agreed.

"You pack and I'll rent the car."

"*Oh là là*, that's my determined girl!"

After just one hour, she came back, quite excited:

"I found a car! It's a bargain! But before you go out there and check it out, let me warn you: the car has its issues."

"How many and what kind of issues?"

"I guess you'll find out anyway. So, I'd better tell you. The floor has some holes in it."

"What?"

"Relax! It's actually not a problem, because the air conditioning is not working. The holes will provide us with free ventilation and..." But before she could say anything else, I jumped in:

"That's a relief. One problem solved. What else?"

"Please, do not interrupt me again! Otherwise, it might take us a while! It's kind of a long list!"

"Long list? Oh, why didn't you say so? Please, take your time. Your words are music to my ears."

"Now, keep calm, don't get so upset! To continue, the seats are broken, the windows won't roll up, the speedometer is stuck on eighty and the trunk won't close. Other than that, it is a perfectly good deal!"

"And I'm sure you already found a way on how to solve all these otherwise minor issues."

"I actually did. To hold the seats up, we'll buy enough bottles of water or beer, whatever your preference is."

"Beer. I fear after such a long day we might desperately need some."

"Beer then. About the speedometer, we'll have to get used to not knowing when we'll get a fine and how many will they be. Not a big deal, right?"

"No, not really. If nothing else, we'll just meet a few Indonesian policemen on our way. Who knows, maybe you'll fall in love, as you wish."

"Maybe...but don't worry, the brakes are working, albeit temporarily."

"Bravo! How I love those good deals of yours!"

And so we rolled.

At the first bump, we lost the window at the back. At the second bump, the radio came out, at the third bump, after seeing a local on his motorcycle laughing and waving at us, we started to smell a different fragrance: that of the fresh manure the car was just sliding on.

After we drove for a few hours, singing and chatting away, Jessica said a bit scared:

"Hey Dora, I don't think the fuel gauge is working."

"So what? I'm sure you have a solution for this as well."

"Don't be mean! It should be simple. We'll have to find a gas station."

"It should be easy, but I haven't seen one since we started driving."

Just when we were close to do what any true traveler does, at least once in his lifetime, namely hitchhike, here it was: not the gas station, just the gas. And it has been there all the way, on every corner, at every turn.

"Dora, what do you think is in those Vodka bottles? It cannot be Vodka. The color is not right. Do you think they might sell gas in them?"

"Gas? In Vodka bottles? Now you have some imagination."

"Me or them? There is only one way to find the answer. Let's go ask."

Whoever said life beats fiction was right. In Vodka bottles or Fanta ones, depending on your preference, stacked on shelves outside people's houses, was the gas. Wasn't it common, expected, assumed? It might have been, but only for the locals.

Other than that, not much worth mentioning happened on our way to Ubud.

Once we arrived, to be on the safe side, we decided to have dinner at a German restaurant. We were both aware of how sick one can get in Asia and Bali was not making an exception. People get food allergies, food poisoning, or even worse, people die on their holidays not of pleasure, but of pain. So for two born and bred Europeans, German standards sounded like the way to go.

But, we were both mistaken. In Asia, even German standards take it a notch down. From the supposedly fresh-caught fish we ate, we both got terribly sick.

"These trips between the bathroom and the bed, do they count as traveling?" Jessica asked after a whole week of torture.

"They could. Just not in the right direction."

"That explains why they don't feel too good."

"Let's go out. It might cheer us up!"

In Ubud, local markets sell everything you know or you would prefer not to. You just have to look in the right place. I wanted to buy a mask; as for Jessica she wanted nothing else more than to go back home. But then, she spotted something and she was back to life.

"Look here. Cock-of-the–rock extravaganza, a phallus made out of hard wood. The guy told me it's good. I mean, good as a present," she rapidly added.

"How would he know?" I giggled.

"How would we know it's not?" Jessica gave me a wink.

"You aren't serious, are you? Don't tell me you want to buy a penis?"

"It comes in all sizes, all shapes, with all the curves included."

"Do they have his size?" I asked, amused about where the whole thing was going.

"If we're talking about who I think we're talking about, namely your famous Stallion, I am pleased to inform you they even have bigger ones."

"Bigger ones? You want to kill me, girl?"

"Kill you? No dear, you got it all wrong! It's for him! It will be his present!"

"One to remind him it was *just sex*," I said, suddenly recalling how much it hurt when, after the first time we made love, he said that to me.

"Yes. Plus, if he didn't know how to keep you, it's entirely his loss!"

"It's always the other one's loss, isn't it?"

"Always! And by the way, you should stop calling him Stallion. It makes him sound more important than he is."

"And how would you call him?"

"Hmmm... I don't know... Scallion? You like scallions, don't you? I bet you like them even more than you like Stallions."

"I love stallions, scallions, sliced lengthwise to bruise the flesh, then chopped and fried slowly," I responded giving her an impish look.

Dora's Journal Notes

- *When something is a good deal, ask yourself for whom.*
- *Get the right size and everything else will fit in.*
- *If you don't like your dream, wake up and go to bed again.*
- *Nightmares qualify as dreams too.*
- *Doubt is what keeps the hope alive.*

CHAPTER 26

WHEN AN INTERVIEW GOING WELL LANDS YOU THE WRONG JOB

I love going for an interview,
Being asked questions that I knew
From the other one last week,
They, trying to find out if I'm a freak,
Hoping in silence I'm a geek,
While I dream of becoming a rich sheik.

BACK FROM BALI, I felt a bit like hanging in midair, waiting for the right push to throw me where I belonged.

One morning, looking in the mirror, I wasn't sure if what I saw was my reflection or some ghost resembling me.

"Why do I feel so down?" I asked myself, starting another conversation with the wiser me.

You don't drink, you don't smoke, and lately you don't get laid! the answer came promptly.

"And since when are these answers to anyone's prayers?"

Since old times?

"I know what I have to do: work. Work hard enough and nothing will matter anymore."

And that's including yourself.

"You have an answer for everything, don't you? You know what we call a person who always has something to add even when there is nothing left to be added?"

Sure, I know: smart.

"Smart indeed. But only in their own eyes."

Like any other eyes would matter...

"So, smarty, how should I prepare for the interviews?"

Have you played hide and seek when you were a child?

"Sure, I did. Back in the old times, kids were playing outside with one another."

An interview follows the same rules. When he starts talking, you start thinking of where to hide and by the time he stops you already have a plan. Then, you take turns. And the one who finds where the other one truly stands, wins. However, most of the time the game is over even before anyone finds anyone.

"What do you mean?"

An interview is a lying game and the winner is he who calls the other's bluff. The candidate adjusts the truth in relation to skills and expectations and, when it comes to rewards and work environment, is followed closely by the employer. It might look like there is a conversation going on, but in reality all it happens is a series of well-rehearsed monologues. Let's take for example the classic questions and some plausible answers:

"What is your weakness?"
True answer: "I am an alcoholic."
Answer given: "I am a workaholic."

"What do you believe to be the biggest challenge you might face in your job?"
True answer: "My boss, followed closely by staying awake."
Answer given: "Once I am committed to a job, I enjoy each challenge on the way and there is nothing which I cannot overcome."

"Where do you see yourself in five years?"
True answer: "On a beach in Hawaii sipping a cocktail and learning to play golf."
Answer given: "Contributing to the prosperity of the company."

"How would you describe yourself?"
True answer: "Messy, tardy, unpredictable, difficult to handle, bossy."
Answer given: "Organized, punctual, easygoing, a good team player."

"Why did you leave your last job?"

True answer: "I got bored or I got sacked for...one or the other."

Answer given: "I felt there was nothing left for me to improve and I was ready for a new challenge."

"What do you like to do in your free time?"

True answer: "Sex. However, I hardly find any energy left for it at the end of another long day of work, which pisses me off."

Answer given: "I am a passionate about my job so whenever I have some free time, I like to read more articles on related topics."

"Don't you think you are overqualified for this position?"

True answer: "Sure, I am. Don't we all think we are?"

Answer given: "No, I think I can learn a lot from working with you."

"What is your leadership style?"

True answer: "Get it all done and done well. Don't bother me!"

Answer given: "I enjoy mentoring people, motivating, and understanding them."

"What is your salary expectation?"

True answer: "A million per year, preferably after tax, will do just fine."

Answer given: "I have heard the position is paid with one hundred thousand per year. But, if it's too much, I am open to negotiations."

"Would you be able to work overtime?"

True answer: "You definitely did not read the last attention span reports. You are lucky if I will be productive for half of the day."

Answer given: "Sure, whenever the company needs me, I will be there."

"Why would you like to work with us?"

True answer: "I have a mortgage to pay; otherwise I would be out of here in no time."

Answer given: "I have always wanted to work in this industry. Working for such a reputable firm will be my dream come true."

"There will be lots of things to learn in this job. Will you be OK with reading more material in your spare time?"

True answer: "No dear, slavery was abolished a long time ago."

Answer given: "Sure, I was just about to ask you about that. I would love to learn more each day and every single weekend."

Whoever said the truth is better than a thousand lies must have been an idiot with suicidal tendencies or one who already knew the truth and was hoping for a lie.

"Sometimes, the truth can be more damaging than a lie."

You'd better go to bed. It's late and you're tired. Tomorrow is another day.

And so, exhausted after such a long conversation with myself, I went to bed.

The following week, dressed for success and keeping the lessons in mind, I went for a few interviews.

It might have been my smile, my knowledge, my attitude or why not, my lies. Whatever it was, it landed me the well-sought-after job. I was working now in one of the biggest law firms in Melbourne, as a junior lawyer. My parents were proud of me, while my grandma thought once again it was all the result of her prayers:

"God is watching over all of us. He listened to my prayers and now you have a job. You just have to get married and you'll be just fine."

"You're the biggest dreamer in our family, Grandma. I wish happiness was so simple," I said to her gently.

For her, what kind of job and what kind of husband I will have were details, never important enough to bother God with them. And if she didn't bother God with them, God didn't bother Himself either.

After a few months of coming face to face with what practicing law really meant, I found out a simple truth about myself: I had no qualms about lying to the ones who wanted to be lied to, but when it came to myself, I was a poor liar.

I had to face the truth: if becoming a lawyer was ever my dream, it was not anymore. I did not enjoy practicing law and the fact that I worked for years and years to get there did not change this simple truth.

But coming to terms with the truth was not as easy as finding it out. Lesson learned: ask only if you really want to know the answer. And this includes the questions you ask yourself.

I called Robert. Whenever I was in trouble, his humor was priceless. Although it was past midnight, he picked up:

"Robert, I have a problem!"

"Just one? Wow! You're lucky."

"It's a big one: I don't want to be a lawyer!"

"That's a relief, sweetie, not a problem. You were not cut out for it anyway. You just had to find out by yourself. I remember having a bit of a discussion a few months back."

His words were soothing. He was not angry with me, did not blame me or call me crazy. If only my parents could have been like that...then, probably I would have woken them up instead of Robert. He continued:

"But did you figure it out what you wanna be?"

"I want to be a writer, a gardener, or even a chef and travel the world!"

"And, what's stoppin' you?" he asked me calmly.

"What's stopping me? Everything. It's just a dream. It was always a dream, a farfetched one this time. Dreams are called dreams, for a reason: they never become reality."

"True, by themselves none become reality. Tell me, when you look at a caterpillar, what do you see?"

"A caterpillar."

"Every Tom, Dick, and Harry sees that. But not me. I see what a caterpillar turns into. I see a butterfly. A dream is like a caterpillar, the only difference is it needs *you* to turn it into a butterfly."

"I wish it would be true, but I doubt it's that simple."

"Hell yeah. Tell me, livin' in Canada wasn't a dream? What about ending up in the sunny land of Oz? Or all those countries you traveled to? Or your most precious dream: becoming a lawyer again. I can still remember that day: it was two weeks after you landed in Canada. You had no job, no money, no relatives, at least none that could count as family, your English was poor, and you were crying on the floor all day long. But one day, you told me: 'I will be a lawyer again. I promise.' That was your dream back then. No one would have given you a chance. But, against all odds, you made it. You found a way. You turned your dream into reality. So what makes the one you have now any different from the others?"

"I don't know."

"You don't know, because there's nothing to know. Daring or less daring, they are all dreams and they can all come true if you have confidence. You must believe in your power, their power, the universe's power. And it will happen."

Robert was right. Stepping down now and playing by the rules felt like a sacrilege, like a sin, like an unforgivable and unforgettable mistake.

"There are no farfetched dreams, sweetie, just illusions about what makes us truly happy. You thought being a lawyer would make you happy. That was your dream, but it was also an illusion because now that you're a lawyer, you aren't happy. Nevertheless, the dream itself came true."

"You're right..."

"Am I not always?"

"My wise terrestrial angel. You always make me laugh."

"Good. I'll send you the bill. People that make others laugh are in high demand nowadays."

"I hope you don't charge in six minutes increments."

"I charge in hugs."

"Then, send me the bill!"

After talking to Robert, I knew, before condemning myself to a life of compromise, I had to listen to my inner call once more, reach for the sky, and follow my dreams. It might not have been a wise thought, but this did not change the truth behind it; it might not have been a safe bet, but neither was my journey so far.

I decided to leave behind the comfort and security of a career in law and plunge again into the unknown, hoping this time my dream would be the right one for me.

Dora's Journal Notes

- *The one who masters his fears, masters his destiny.*
- *We are all scared, but while some become heroes, others become victims.*
- *If you want realistic answers, ask realistic questions.*
- *A person's past will be more relevant than their promises for the future.*
- *In life, we all have to have at least one person to be fully honest with and if we don't start with ourselves, then no one else will have the honor.*
- *Knowing that what makes us happy is difficult to accomplish, should not be a reason to accept what makes us miserable.*
- *If the dream which you once had does not feel right anymore, don't be afraid to start chasing a new one.*
- *We should not fear our dreams will not come true; instead, we should fear they might not be the right ones for us.*
- *Sometimes, the fastest way to get rid of an obsession is to go along with it.*

CHAPTER 27

MISTRESSES AND OTHER COMPLICATIONS

If you feel you're growing old,
Not in the mood because it's cold,
Getting grumpy, even frumpy,
Far too sensitive and jumpy,

It might be it's not your year
Or you just lost someone dear,
Maybe the stars did not align
And you were born in the wrong sign.
But, if you ask me, I would say
You need LOVE to come your way!

I HAVE ALWAYS WONDERED what is the purpose of a serious relationship, a casual fling, or a one-night stand?

Back then, we might not know it, and later we might not want to think of it. But I firmly believe that each person who passes through our life, in a more or less romantic manner, is a messenger who tries to teach us something.

Some might teach us how we give, others how to receive; how to ask or how to refuse; how to beg for more or how to live in denial, how to let go or how to pursue. Some might show us how low we can go, others how high we can reach.

The next story is about a bit of all that.

Louis was not another regular guy, but the owner of the company Jessica was working for. He was not Caucasian, but Asian, not single, but married, not her age, but twenty-five years older, not handsome, but caring, not rich, but not too far behind. Not sure which one of those attributes could be the major theme of any gossiping, but something tells me all could play an important part. However, for her, none mattered too much.

She was not seeing his wrinkles, but his smiling eyes. She was not thinking of the age gap between them, but of how happy they were together.

The fact that he was married and she was his mistress never made her feel less worth it.

She never tricked him or seduced him; their feelings came naturally and manifested as such.

She came in, because he opened his heart and he opened it because he wanted to.

For me, their relationship will always represent the proof that when love is genuine, boundaries such as age, position, or marital status do not matter. But that was just me.

"The whole thing is a mess. I'm a mess. Or maybe because I'm a mess, the whole thing is a mess. He's my boss," Jessica said to me between tears one beautiful sunny morning.

"He won't be if you fire him. I mean if he fires you. Plus, it's wonderful for a change. Usually, in any relationship the woman is the boss."

"Ha-ha! Fire me? Broken hearted, broke, sure, why not? Please God, give me all your blessings."

"C'mon now. That wouldn't be too bad. You could always find another job. But you might not find one like him. Will he ever get a divorce?"

"A divorce? He's Chinese. For them, saving face is all that matters. They might have changed countries, but the identity of a person doesn't stand in their passport my dear friend, but in their heart."

"He might lose his face, but regain his peace," I said gently.

"I once asked him if he didn't think love is an untamed creature and marriage should be its servant, not its master. You know what he said?"

"No."

"He said, 'What about duty?'"

"There are dreams, there is love and then comes duty and they are all gone. But I guess the question is not what the one in love thinks, but what the one left behind feels. For the master likes the cage, but the bird will always hate it."

"His wife doesn't feel anything. She has no idea about what is happening."

"She doesn't know or she doesn't want to know?"

"Who cares? All I care is one thing: I'll always remain his mistress."

"In life we can all be mistresses, wives, concubines, or partners, but what truly matters is if we are loved and love back. The rest is just a game of circumstances."

"It's hurting me, him and everyone else. I'm committing a crime, the biggest I could commit: I'm sabotaging my own happiness. He's married and if I were smart I'd look for a single guy so I can get married too."

"So, that's how it goes, does it? First, we check his marital status and then all the rest."

"Yes, every woman who has some decency, some ethics does that."

"Aren't you a bit tough on yourself? I wish everyone would agree on what is moral and what is not, on what is right and what is wrong. But the irony is, no matter what we're doing, there will always be someone, somewhere, criticizing us or despising us."

"And the worse is, when that someone is us."

"If that's what you think, why not put an end to it? You might not have had a choice when you fell for him, but you do have a choice now. The wounds will heal in time, he'll regain his peace, and maybe you'll find the long lasting love you so much desire."

"One day I will. But, for now, my heart cannot let go, not today and not tomorrow. For now, I am in love. He is in love. We are in love."

"And the rest...?"

"The rest? I hope they are in love too."

Despite her light humor, I could feel and see her torment. There were no winners. They were both losers in their own way. The only winner was love. And they knew it. Whether they wanted to know it, this was a different question. Same as his wife.

For one year, they were together. And every day of that year they were happy and also wrecked by guilt.

They knew it would end one day, but each day they hoped that wouldn't be the day. They did not live in denial; they lived in hope.

But, in the end, the fears conquered, the preconceptions won, the still small voice reasoned, and they broke up. The reason was not the age difference, but their fear of it. Not his love for his wife, but his fear of losing face. Not the lack of affection, but the power of duty. Their separation was not an unhappy ending, but simply an inevitable change. It was the chance they chose to give to themselves to regain their peace.

Dora's Journal Notes

- *If love happens with whom you wish, when you wish, and where you wish, then it might not be love, but calculated infatuation.*
- *Be ashamed for hating someone, not for loving someone.*
- *Marriage is not a prison, but the house of love. When love is gone, the house crumbles and marriage becomes obsolete.*
- *There is no triangle. In love there are always only two people.*
- *Infatuation sees the obstacles; love sees ways around them.*
- *Divorce is a small price to pay for having another shot at happiness.*
- *The difference between a man and a gentleman is that while both want it, the first will ask for it, while the second will make you ask for it.*

CHAPTER 28

A ROSE IN AMSTERDAM

In search for happiness I went astray
To learn my lessons, play and pray,
But here I was time and again,
Her blood was running through my veins,
And so, I went to say Hello,
Bongiorno, Buna or Bonjour,
To mother Europe: love toujours!

WHENEVER I NEED INSPIRATION and courage, I travel: for a few days, for a few weeks, for a few months, for whatever it takes.

I travel to confront and forget my old worries, fears, and even hopes and forge new ones, to shed my own skin and let a new layer take over, to find the answers I am looking for, the path which I lost.

I travel because when I travel I feel life is beautiful.

Sometimes I go far away, to meet cultures different than my own, to learn words I can barely pronounce. Other times, I miss home, I miss Europe.

Europe is my old friend, my beloved mother, my ideal lover. It's my refuge, my escape from the storms, my place to rejoice and to rest.

And now, after I quit my job and I was unsure of what I wanted to do next, it was time for me to pay it a visit. A long three months visit.

Like always, I did not know if I would find in Europe whatever answers I was looking for, but something told me I had to go. Jessica's mourning process was also taking a toll on her and so, she decided to join me for the first two weeks.

"Wake up, sleepy head!" Jessica screamed at me.

"Just go away! I was dreaming."

"Like it wouldn't be enough you dream during the day, now you have to dream during the night too! What were you dreaming about?"

"We were renting a small house with a boat beside the river in Giethoorn, the Venice of Holland. After a delicious breakfast in an open-air cafe on the shores of the Bosphorus, we went hiking around Lake Como in Italy, then straight into the Ice Caves in Austria. We spent the afternoon swimming and watching the sunset over the wineries in Corniglia, Cinque Terre, listening to the loud, lively Italians. We went for lunch in Salzburg to have a garlic soup and then to a Parisian fancy cafe which serves a delicious beef tartar. We spent the night on a boat in Monaco, and fell asleep caressed by the waves crashing on the shore."

"Wow! Weren't we busy? You got the first bit almost right."

"What do you mean?" I said, trying hard to wake up while my head was spinning. Then, I saw on the table some cheese with figs and mustard.

"Welcome to Amsterdam! Welcome to free love, to avant-garde music and art, to Cannabis Cup and intriguing sex shops, to red cubicles and flamboyant women, to narrow canals and gay pride," Jessica exclaimed turning on the twenty-four-seven unlimited porn channel. "We arrived yesterday morning and you have slept almost twenty four hours. It must have been the jet lag! But now that you're finally awake, you'd better stay like that! As long as I'm here, we'll have a blast!"

For the next two weeks, we roamed the streets of Amsterdam, waking up before the roosters and collapsing late at night with a new list of must see places for the following day.

"I know why all those people are happy here! It's the pills!" she told me one day, happy like a baby finally catching Santa in the act.

"The contraception pills, you mean?" I made fun of her statement.

"Those too. But look here, miracle pills!" she pointed to a store displaying hundreds of pills colorfully packed. "Wow! That's a lot of pills! Let's go in! We might need a few!"

"Knowing which one is the one for us will be tricky though!"

Holding a shiny package, Jessica started to read out loud: "If you never want to get off the sofa, this is for you!"

"Why someone would never want to get off the sofa?"

"I don't know. It looks like the pill promotes a blissful slow painless death. Not the right one for us. But, look here: *Aquarius, the cosmic experience.* Aren't you an Aquarius? That might explain your hot episodes with your Stallion."

"Guilty as charged. And if you're so curious, just try me. You might not need this pill after all," I said laughing at her.

"If I'll try you, I'll definitely not need that pill over there!" she laughed back pointing to the contraception shelves.

"But, just in case I might be too much for you, you might need a condom! So, which one should it be? The black cactus with spines all over for intense pleasure or itchiness or the daring dragon? Or maybe you fancy a tiny mouse for your future husband? The bicycle and the windmill if he is Dutch, the pumpkin or the golf ball if he is an American lost in the clouds?" I asked, showing her the tons of condoms coming in all kinds of size, shape and design to protect the knight for the night.

"Perhaps the Christmas tree with the elk for festive occasions or the romantic heart condom in case he decides to propose to me in the heat of the moment?"

"Why not the one with the clock if he's married with his business or just with someone else?"

"If that's the case, I won't need a condom at all. Anyway, how could we possibly know the right size?"

"Put it this way: if we buy a condom that's too small for him, we chose the right guy. But, if we buy one that's too big, in this case, maybe we should skip the affair altogether."

"And then, I'll have no choice than coming back to you, for that *Aquarius cosmic experience.*"

"You got it! Behind any lesbian stands an impotent man!"

"Look here, *How to use a condom: keep the condom away from the light and heat.*"

"Why? Will it melt? What should one do when in the middle of a poppy field, in one of those hot summer days when all you need is love? Wait for those cold nights of winter and in the meantime keep it in the fridge?"

"Hahaha! Dora, listen to the next one, it's even less enticing: *Don't have intercourse with a condom for too long.*"

"Define too long. Plus, we're usually in no danger for this to happen..."

"Unfortunately... You don't like Woody Allen's movies, right?" Jessica asked me, suddenly changing the topic.

"No, not really. I feel either depressed or stupid after watching any of them. None of those states of mind are quite a happy ending for me."

"You might start to like him more. Read here what the maestro said: '*Is sex dirty? Only when it's done right.*'"

"Or with the shoes on," I responded.

"Or another one: '*Don't knock masturbation. It's sex with someone you love.*'"

"Or you hate!" I fired back.

"You really don't like Woody Allen!"

"I told you...I dislike with the same passion I like."

"Then I'd better make sure you continue to like me, Miss Aquarius!"

"You'd better, Miss Leo!"

On our last day in Amsterdam, we were walking back home when we saw a man in the distance leaving a red rose and an envelope on our doorstep. Then, he left in a hurry.

We ran and full of curiosity and excitement opened the envelope: "For Dora, Never give up on love," signed: Tomás. There was no last name, no address, no telephone number.

We followed him to a small café where violins were playing and baskets of colorful flowers were hanging by the door. But we were too late. He was gone. We lost him.

"Leave a message for him with the waitress. He might return. You never know, he might be your next stallion," Jessica said, amused of the whole thing.

"I don't want another stallion!"

"Then tell him what you want! Tell him he has *to feel right* with the emphasis on *feel*," she continued, starting to moan softly in my ears.

"You're a pain, has anybody told you?"

"And you're a hotty disguised as a nun! Do it and let's get it over with! Tomorrow when I'll go back to Australia, I want to know I left you in good hands!"

And so I did. I left my message to him with the waitress, just in case he might return:

"I don't just date. I'm looking for my soul mate. I don't pamper! I don't build and ruin dreams! I am what you see! I think what you hear! I can't stand rogues or clowns! I look for a real man, one who admits his mistakes and brags about his achievements, who knows what he wants and is not afraid to admit it; who has the courage to love and the strength to leave when love is gone!

Come and meet me! You will either adore me or hate me! You will either be sick of me or never tired of me! Let's plunge together into the unknown, and emerge forever victorious! I will take the TGV tomorrow to Paris. Dora"

And this is when a new chapter of my life began.

Dora's Journal Notes

- *Sometimes, a rose on our doorstep seems to be all we struggle for.*

CHAPTER 29

PARIS: LA VIE EN ROSE

You are shy or talk too much,
You are blushing, but would like to touch,
You forget what you're about to say,
Or, just ramble in a nonsensical way,
You keep hoping a smoochy will follow,
You want to eat, but you cannot swallow,
Don't worry my friend, take it in stride,
It's love at first sight and you cannot hide!

ALL SWEATY, carrying my numerous mostly untouched suitcases, with my nails half-done like usual, in a colorful dress and with my beloved scarf around my neck, looking quite helpless, but nevertheless sure of myself, I arrived to the train station.

Wherever I go, all train stations look quite the same to me: crowded, noisy, smelling like international perfume bottle day or stinking of cigarette smoke, with people running around in a hurry, while others clinging to each other whisper their goodbyes. I hate them all and the one in Amsterdam was no exception.

I jumped into my carriage: number seven, my lucky number. I quickly sat down, feeling like I had just escaped from a calamity and I could finally relax.

I was getting ready to start reading the latest book of Malcolm Gladwell, when I heard a man's voice:

"*Bonjour! Comment ça va?*"

I lifted my eyes and I saw him: the guy with the envelope, the guy with the rose, the same guy, my one and only Prince Charming.

"*Bonjour! Ça va bien, merci,*" I replied a bit nervous. hoping his English was better than my French.

He was tall, with dark blue eyes, beautiful big hands, dressed in a pale blue casual shirt.

"I got your message. A bit intriguing, I have to say. I found the coincidence remarkable: I am expected in Paris tomorrow for an international cooking contest. I'm a chef. I'm sorry, let me introduce myself. My name is Tomás."

"Your accent, I cannot tell from where you are..."

"I live in Buenos Aires, but I spend most of the year traveling around, organizing cooking events, teaching men how to cook. In other words, making the life of women easier. And you?"

"Me? Oh, me... I'm from Melbourne, Australia."

He had a warm genuine smile, one that I could look at for hours. His eyes were kind, his moves were smooth, elegant, and his voice, although a bit gruff, was not commanding, but rather mysterious and tender. His sexy, Latino accent was instantly making me happy and dreamy.

We started talking about everything and nothing in particular. I wanted to listen to him, but also to speak; I wanted to know his dreams, his passions, the places he adored to go to, but I also wanted to show him who I was, brag about my achievements, convince him I was worth knowing too. To make it even worse, or even better, I was laughing at everything he was saying, like a silly schoolgirl.

After just a few hours, I wanted to touch him or at least move closer to him, and an inexplicable excitement and curiosity were taking over me.

But I was too aware of how unconventional, maybe even weird, all that was.

Instead, I asked him:

"Would you like me to show you Paris? It can get a bit confusing if you've never been before."

While the words were coming freely from my mouth, my brain was under attack by a million of other thoughts:

What's in your head, girl? It's your first time in Paris too. If he says yes, you'll look like a fool.

"And if I don't ask, I'll feel like an idiot."

True. Better a fool than an idiot.

Like he could hear the conversation and didn't want to prolong my torture, Tomás said:

"I've been to Paris before. But, seeing Paris with you will be totally different. Let's meet tomorrow. We might just find what Paris is so famous for."

My heart stopped beating. What did he mean by "what Paris is so famous for"? Did he mean what I think he meant? Paris, the city of love. I was too shy and scared to ask. Instead, I simply replied:

"Yes, we'll make sure to *tour* Eiffel."

"Yes, Tour Eiffel makes Paris famous. But other things do too," he said giving me again that beautiful smile who was cutting through all my defenses.

"Focus, Dora! Don't lose focus!" I said to myself determined this time not to let my heart take over my head. "You came to Europe to find your answers. Take a deep breath, look away from his blue eyes, and make sure you go to bed alone!"

But as soon as I said it, my nagging inner voice came up with one of its smarty comments:

What if love will show you the answer? And what if he will show you what love really is? What if he will be your friend and your stallion?

"What if, this is what kills us. What if...There is only one way to find out."

Confronting my fears and looking straight into his eyes, I answered:

"I'd love to see together with you all the things that make a trip to Paris unforgettable. Who knows? Together, we might discover much more than we already know."

"The pleasure will be all mine, mi hermosa."

The next few weeks were the best of my life. The most serene and the most romantic. They were complete.

With him, I felt an overwhelming peace coming over me, a sense of belonging and some sort of familiarity hard to explain. Everything between us felt natural; there was no angst, no signs telling me I got to beware.

His words were speaking my mind and my mind could understand and follow his.

Something beyond my comprehension was telling me he was the one I have been looking for, waiting for, wanting for, all that time.

Sure, it might have been great if he was living in Australia and sure it would have been great to have all the time in the world to know him better. But, love is an untamable creature. It does not come when you want or where you want and the best you could hope for is the person to be the right one for you. I guess, to have some control over it, one can just start by relinquishing control and have faith.

"Would you like to go to the Louvre?" he asked one day.

"Would you?" I asked back thinking of how much I dreaded going to museums.

"No, not really."

"Birds of the same feather flock together."

"What?"

"Nothing. Just thinking out loud, my dear dearest."

"The thing is I've never been a fan of museums. What can one do inside of an empty haunted house, albeit it's a palace? Admire dead art created by dead people and listen to stories of the past."

"Art is precious and even more so when it becomes antique. People pay fortunes for a piece of the kettle that touched for a second the hands of Louis III," I teased him.

"And I'll pay fortunes too, but just so your hands can touch our kettle each morning," he replied, giving me a soft kiss. "I know we have to learn from the past if we don't want to repeat its mistakes. But, it's never only about knowing something, is it? It has to make you tick; it has to resonate with you."

"It has to feel right!"

"*Précisément!* Between admiring Gold French furniture, chandeliers, painted murals on ceilings, judging a past whose complete tale I will never know and walking the beautiful streets of Montmartre and talking to contemporaneous painters, I'll always choose the latter. I want to feel the pulse of the moment, to meet the artists of my time, to listen to stories which are happening as we speak or just donate a coin for the poor blind man whose heart is still ticking."

"Life is for the living!" I said back.

"And Paris for the ones in love!" Tomás said before kissing me passionately.

Embraced, I, dressed with a colorful orange dress matching my brown no-heel sandals, and he, handsome as always in his navy shirt, we walked out the hotel to face another day in Paris, the city of love.

I never wanted to leave Europe. I was afraid once we would go back, me to Australia and him to Argentina, all we would have left would be just another memory, albeit a beautiful one. As much as I was fond of memories, some of them I wanted to keep living and he was one of them.

I tried to imagine myself immigrating for the third time in eight years. Only thinking of everyone's reaction made me smile. I knew I could not do it again. The last few years were not easy and I was tired: tired of studying, of figuring out things from scratch, of making new friends, tired of waking up in a new place with a new adventure waiting for me around each corner.

I knew from my experience that, for him, moving to Australia would be a great sacrifice. So, if it was ever to happen, it had to come from him. He had to want to take the step badly enough so, if things got rough he wouldn't want to go back. Whether or not we would be together forever and ever was entirely in his hands. As for me, all I could do was trust he would make the right decision for both of us.

Dora's Journal Notes

- *While nothing is more common that a discussion about love, nothing is rarer than true love.*
- *Opportunities come, but rarely stay. We are lucky to have them, brave to take them, and wise to know which ones to pick.*

CHAPTER 30

WHEN FRIENDSHIP MARRIES LUST

Isn't Lust the most primal and sought after love?
Doesn't it calm the nerves and bring peace like a
white dove?
Don't we all want to have a share of it each day?
Don't we all hope it is here to stay?

WITH SLOW, LASCIVIOUS MOVES, in the dim light of the candles, I took off my clothes: first the bright yellow skirt, then the deep red blouse and the belt and finally I slipped the straps of the bra off my shoulders. "Let the senses guide and the imagination flow, Dora," I could hear the voice telling me.

Despite feeling a bit shy, I wanted to do it this way. I took a deep breath and continued: I opened the bra clasp, letting it fall on the floor. I took off my panties. In my high-heeled shoes, standing naked, in front of the one I loved, I said:

"Voilà, monsieur! Je suis toi! Pour toujours ou pour un jour. Parce que je t'aime, pour toujours et à jamais."

"I could not imagine anything more beautiful than you, my love!"

"Then, you don't have too much imagination, *señor*," I replied, smiling. "Having said that, I might admit you're right!"

"So humble!"

"Just stating the obvious!"

"You can cast a spell over whoever dares to watch you too closely, for too long."

"I just have to cast a spell on you."

"You don't have to worry about that, missy!"

I could see in his eyes that, the most basic of the instincts was taking over and for a second I could hear his pulse hammering through his veins.

"I want to grab you so badly! I want to pull you so close to me so no one can tell us apart. I want to rub my unshaven face on your delicate pale skin until it becomes all red and all you want is for me to press my hips into yours. I want to make love to you now and forever. I love you, Dora!"

"I love you too, Tomás!" I said, feeling my cheeks getting red.

And then it happened. The miracle happened: my love was finally my lover and my lover was finally my love. And we were one.

After we made love, bewildered, we sat in silence for a while.

"A penny for your thoughts," I went first.

"No thoughts. Just amazement. I'm amazed by the beauty of you all: by your green eyes, the contour of your lips, your messy bouncy hair, the shapes of your body. I'm amazed by the way you make love: so free and passionate, so warm and sensual. I'm amazed of who you are, of your twisted mind, your humor, your quick wit, your heart," he said touching first my eyes, my hair, and then my lips. "You're a beautiful woman, and I love you so much!"

"You're the best lover I've ever had!" I said a bit surprised and happy.

"Clearly you did not try many!"

"Clearly I did not try the right ones!" I said thinking of Stallion. Then, I continued:

"It's not this sex part."

"Making love you mean. This is what sex becomes for me when I'm with you. It's pure, shared love. It's art. The most beautiful of all."

"Yes," I said, thinking of Stallion again. The distinction was making perfect sense. "It's not only how you make me feel when you're inside me, it is everything. You're everything, without being special in any particular way. You're quite an ordinary guy, you know that?"

"I'm listening."

"I mean you're not extravagantly rich or handsome or who knows what. You're just an ordinary, simple guy. You actually lack a lot of the things I imagined the one I'll love will have."

"That's a profound discussion! And I'm not sure whether it's the most flattering either!"

"You don't dance, you don't sing in the car, not even in the shower and you don't talk much."

"On the other hand, you, little chatter box, are doing all of them for both of us!"

"But, being with you just feels right. No matter what we're doing, with you I feel at ease. I can trust you; I can confide in you; I can count on you. There is nothing I'd be afraid or shy to tell you! On top of it, you make me die with pleasure, mister!"

"Die with pleasure, you say? *I just died in your arms tonight...*" he started to sing.

"Scorpions! Oh, you are a terrible singer!"

"Good enough for you to recognize the song! And now, that we're in the declaration phase, allow me to share my thoughts and feelings with you."

"I thought you did. But nothing will please me more than hearing all of it once more!"

"The most important things don't hurt to be told twice, do they? So, allow me to start. I love you! *Je t'aime! Te iubesc! Te Amo!* I love your natural beauty, delicate figure, soft baby skin. I love the way you are, shy but daring, fearful but curious, proud, but so easy going. And because I love you, each morning I want to be the one making you moan for the first time, groan of pleasure for the first time, scream for more for the first time. Each day I want to let myself be possessed by this uncontrollable desire for your beautiful, responsive body. And each day I want to protect you, to have you by my side, to help you follow your dreams, to be your friend, your confidant, your mentor, your partner! I want to be everything for you and I want you to be everything for me."

"What will happen when this holiday is over?" I asked him giving voice to my worse fear.

"Wherever you'll go, I'll go. As long as we're together I'll be the happiest and luckiest guy in the world. I know you're right. I'm not the most impressive guy. I don't drive a fancy car and I don't have a big mansion by the lake. Or not yet. I'm not a lawyer, a doctor or some gifted businessman you can show off with. And I'm definitely not the most handsome guy going after you. You, on the other hand, are perfect. You are bright, beautiful, fun to be with, you make love like a goddess, you cook better than a chef, you are any man's dream! You can make any man fall in love with you! Although Prince William might be unavailable!"

"There's always his brother!"

"Indeed, leave alone all the rest of unmarried royal heads!"

"But I want you, silly!"

"This time you are the silly one, missy! I'm just a terrible lucky fellow! But, as your faithful servant now and forever, your wish is my command! So, if you want me, there is nothing in the world that will stop me from being with you. Jobs, countries, houses are all details. Together we'll figure them all out. The big question is: will you marry me, Dora?"

"I might..." I paused.

I could see his face turning from red to pale and his eyes changing from clear blue to dark blue.

"Yes, I will marry you Tomás, my ordinary, beautiful, silly lover and friend! Just as a side note before we tie the knot, two things: first, how did you know my name was Dora when you left me the note in Amsterdam?"

"Remember the condom store in Amsterdam selling ecstasy pills too? When you were there with your friend, I was there too. There was something about you that made my heart skip a beat. It never happened to me before."

"Thank heavens. Otherwise, I'd be talking to your spirit now."

"Ha! Don't interrupt me. I'm really making an effort here. So, I heard Jessica calling you Dora. All day I had been following you. And, oh my God, didn't you two walk a lot? I followed you down to the Diamonds Museum, the main plaza, even to that terrible Turkish restaurant you guys had lunch at. I could definitely have skipped that part. I got a terrible tummy ache after eating there. But love requires sacrifice. I even followed you to your house. All the time I was hoping for a chance to talk to you alone. As it did not happen, I trusted my instincts and left you that note. And now, here we are."

"A toast for your instincts! May they be all the time as right as they were on that day!"

"A toast for your courage to respond to me! May your adventurous spirit take you as far as you'd like to go and always a step further! What was the second thing?"

"I lied to you."

"I know you've never been to Paris before," he said calmly.

"How did you know?"

"The maps on your bed? Your desire not to let any stone unturned and see each thing on the postcards? Pick whichever you like. Plus, I let you alone two times and in both cases you got lost."

"Don't worry about getting lost. It's an old dear habit of mine," I said, while the image of Stallion suddenly came back to my mind. Just that this time, I did not feel pain or confusion. This time I felt relief. Leaving him was the right thing to do. I was happy. And I hoped wherever he was and whoever he was with, he was at least as happy as I was.

Dora's Journal Notes

- *Love is the strongest when friendship marries insatiable lust.*
- *Save the ruins of the past only after saving the children of the future.*
- *The answers found in books are a bit like the daily horoscope. Some of them might be right for you, others only for your neighbor. Get your own from living your own reality.*
- *Surrender to love and love will surrender to you.*

CHAPTER 31

A KNOT, SOME WORDS AND WE'RE ALL DONE

First they were two: Adam and Eve,
Then, she bit that apple and took a sick leave,
One that will always in history remain,
As the longest sick leave ever to blame.
From the Garden of Eden they were thrown deep
Into the Land of Reality to become the black sheep.
Surrounded by fears, opponents, and rum,
Adam decided there was nowhere to run.
And so, in madness he went on to propose
And as a sign of true love he gave her a rose.
Eve did accept and showed her goodwill
By giving him children instead of taking the pill.
But one day, drunk, tired and covered in debt,
Adam said to his soon to be engaged spoiled brat:
My dear son, she might look slim,
Her parents rich and her smile brim,
But she might also not remain as such,
Will you then wanna marry her that much?
If you still do, and I hope you will
God bless this old, wonderful thrill!

YOU CAN LOVE SOMEONE in many ways, and tell them you love them in even more, but in the end what really matters is what your love means to them. Is it worth anything? Does it make them happy?

I always thought that to love and be loved back is the ultimate source of happiness and energy. Maybe it's a naive and an old fashioned way of thinking and today's world is much more complicated than that.

But for me, his love will always be what the peaks are to the mountain, what the wings are to the butterfly, what the shade is to the forest, the water to the river, the sun to the day, the stars to the night, the flowers to the pasture, the words to the poem, the freedom to the bird, the ashes to Phoenix, the flamboyant colors to the rooster. It is Everything.

Between the Romanian Carpathian Mountains lies Transylvania, the land of medieval castles and painted monasteries, ancient caves and salt mines, tall peaks and deep valleys, steep gorges and glacial lakes, the land of Vlad the Impaler – Dracula, the "land beyond the forest."

In Transylvania, time is frozen; the grass is still cut with the scythe and you can still see horse drawn carts with beautiful girls giggling as they sit on top of haystacks, and people wearing traditional costumes each Sunday morning on their way to church.

There, at the edge of an ancient forest, surrounded by bushes of wild blueberries, in the smell of pine trees, with me dressed in a simple white dress hand-embroidered with red cotton threads, wearing traditional leather sandals tied around my feet with a long, narrow strip and a wildflower crown on my head, Tomás and I said our vows. He was the best choice not in the whole world, but of my life.

"I cannot promise you I will love you forever and ever. Eternity is not ours to promise. But I do promise to love you each day I will tell you that."

"Honesty! Let's see if I can match that. I cannot promise I will make you happy. Happiness is a game of two. But I do promise I will try harder each day and if won't succeed I will set you free."

"Freedom! Hard one to beat! I promise to stand by you in joy and sorrow, because next to you, my nest is not a prison and I am not an inmate, but a happy traveler through life and marriage."

"Commitment! The most difficult part for some, easy when one has *you*. If in heaven He is our God, on Earth you are my Goddess."

"Magic! It's what makes a city like Paris from grey to beautiful and an evening on the grass watching the lights of tour Eiffel from ordinary to quite special. I promise to be by your side, to believe in your dreams and never doubt they will become reality."

"Support! Without it, lust is in vain. I promise to show you the way, but let you find your own, to be shield and sword, your slave and master, your surgeon and healer."

"Friendship! The most powerful bond! I promise to always be myself: a dictator with the face of an angel lecturing you whenever you will make a boo-boo just so I can make you a better man."

"Genuineness! Where else you would like to go when at home you can be yourself? I promise to love you when you are mad and even more when you scream for more!"

"Lust! The spark that turns friendship into love! I promise to love you even more when the screaming part happens!"

"I love you because a woman like you leaves no other option than to love her."

"And I love you because a man like you leaves no other option than to love him back."

"I take you, Dora, as my wedded wife, and I promise to love, honor, and respect you; to be faithful to you; and not to forsake you until death do us part. So help me God, one in the Holy Trinity, and all the Saints. Never be less. Always flower. Always wild."

"I take you, Tomás as my wedded husband, and I promise to love, honor, and respect you; to be faithful to you; and not to forsake you until death do us part. So help me God, one in the Holy Trinity, and all the Saints."

"Amen!"

"Not amen, silly! *Amin*! We're in Romania! Let's go have lunch! These vows are making me hungry!"

"Yes, dear!"

"And then, I need a shag!"

"Yes, dear!"

"And a good night's sleep!"

"Yes, dear!"

"Stop this *"yes, dear"* thing! Try the next one: I am sorry, dear."

"Yes, dear! I am sorry, dear!" he said and we burst out laughing.

Dora's Journal Notes

- *If you have to ask for love, you'd better look somewhere else.*
- *In a relationship, security without freedom values nothing, but freedom paired with security is everything.*
- *Where true love exists, marriage is optional.*
- *As lovers, not soldiers, we should do things out of love not out of duty.*
- *Life of a man: the wife is always right and when she's not, his mother is.*

CHAPTER 32

One Question: Will You Pick Up When Your Dreams are Calling?

I dream of flowers yellow and blue
Surrounding a red house and a canoe,
With parrots that squawk be it sunny or rain,
With books in my hands picking my brain,

Making a soup from my own veggie patch,
Writing a tale about match and mismatch,
Travel the seas and the world in between,
Touching Antarctica and a croc's skin.

Growing older with him by my side,
Laughing at my first Wonderland ride,
Listening to his jokes always funny and true,
While we keep philosophizing on what's old and
what's new.

WE ALL START IN LIFE WITH DREAMS. Most of us, on the way, give them up, temporarily or permanently. We might call it reality check, but it could be just lack of faith, determination, or courage. We might come to terms with it and see it as a happy adjustment or we might always have a tear in our eyes and regard it as a painful failure.

But, there will always be some, who will believe in their dreams and will pursue them no matter what it would take. They will walk the way from impossible to possible, sometimes running, other times crawling, but always moving forward. God, fairies, witches will help them as long as they will not give up too soon or too easy. If, in the end, their dreams will not come true, it will be less important, because what truly matters is that they went through life smiling, in harmony with themselves and not denying what they are or what they want. They gave themselves the chance and regrets will not haunt their old days.

"You've led quite an incredible life. Did you ever have a moment when you just wanted to make it simple for yourself, give up on your dreams, and just be content with what life throws at you?" Tomás asked me, on our last evening in Romania.

"No. For me, reaching for the sky is the only way to find happiness and be content. However, many times, frustrated, I've wondered why it has to be so goddamn complicated."

"So what? You hoped the obstacles will get tired of you and go away before you'll get tired of them?"

"Obstacles never go away. We just get more fit. I think life is more a sport of endurance than a sprint, don't you think? If we don't lose focus sooner or later, we all get there."

"That's a big *if.* It's easy to lose focus and turn around when no one believes in your dreams."

"But you believe in them. And it's the only thing that matters; the only thing that can bring your forward or stop you in your tracks. You must give yourself a chance. Sometimes, the people close to us can be the toughest obstacles standing between us and our dreams. There will be times when those people will bluntly tell you to wake up and face the reality. And that's fine. After all, it's their experience, their belief, their approach to life. We should respect it and maybe consider it. But ultimately, the decision should be ours."

"But what would you say to them? What did you say to your parents? I'm sure there were arguments."

"My response would be simple: the only reality I have to face is of having dreams which ask to be fulfilled."

"True."

"It's not easy. It took me years to learn to take sole ownership of my dreams. I see them as my children. No one can understand or love them more than I do. And no one will suffer more than I will if they won't be nurtured. Every person has their own dreams, their own children to foster. Asking them to understand and love mine, the same way I do, is like asking a stepmother to care for your children as much as you do. She can try and succeed to some degree, but the bond will never be the same."

"True again."

"I'm the master of my dreams, they give me power and I give them back faith. I create my dreams and they create my reality."

"You are the master of your dreams...What was your dream when you left Romania?"

"I had many dreams. Some were mine, others I thought they were mine. But one was above all. I wanted each day of my life to fall in love with life. That was my main goal, my most precious wish, my urge."

"If I had a magic wand and I could fulfill you one wish now which one would it be?"

"One wish? That's not difficult at all. I wish to be granted more wishes," I said laughing.

"And I wish you wouldn't be so greedy."

"Now you are the one wasting your wishes. Instead of wishing others to be different, you'd better wish you'd be different."

"Me? Different? But I love myself! The others are the ones annoying! I'm a poor soul misunderstood, mistreated..."

"Yah, yah, yah. I know. I feel the same way. And I bet every other person walking on this Earth feels the same at least once a day!" I said giving him a pat on the back.

"Maybe it's time for an International Sorrow day! But, be it: you win. I will grant you all the wishes."

"All of them?"

"I mean the ones that make sense."

"Make sense to you or to me? Definitely it's time for an International Be and Let be day!"

"You might not like it, but you are a lawyer. You never give up, do you?"

"I give up, but only if it makes sense. To me, of course," I said laughing.

"Which never does!"

"Exactly my point!"

"C'mon, I wanna know. Open up!"

"There isn't much to know really. My dreams were always as simple and humble, as complex and daring. I want to have a small house and a big garden. The house will be cozy and simple, full of colors and warmth, a place to rejoice, relax and dream. On the walls, I'll have portraits bought from my trips all over the world. Each painting will have his own beautiful story to share for the ones with a big heart, an open mind and a free spirit. The garden will be full of flowers and veggies, with some chickens running around chased by a determined, horny rooster and two lovely dogs running after a lazy cat, but always coming back empty handed."

"Can they be Border Collies?"

"What else?" I replied, smiling.

"We'll start the day with a long breakfast on the terrace, watching the parrots chattering loudly about the last weather report brought by a raven from the neighboring kookaburra."

"And I'll earn my living writing about the beauty of this universe, the miracle of love, the power of dreams, the mystery of witchery and the energy of our thoughts. My books will make people smile and will give them back the confidence they have lost or the strength to do what deep in their heart they know has to be done."

"What about me? Where do I fit in the picture?"

"You, my imperfect beautiful creature, will travel the world with me, from the Andes to the Amazon, along the Danube to the Rhine, from Utah to Sedona."

"That's a busy adventurous life!"

"Plenty of time to rest afterwards!"

"You'd hope so!"

"Are you in or out?"

"In! In! Take me in!" Tomás said sliding up his hands beneath my silk red blouse.

Then, a bit surprised, he went on:

"That's my woman! You never wear a bra!"

"I live to challenge and be challenged, mister!"

"And I live to devour every single inch of you!"

A few months later, after Tomás moved to Melbourne, we rented a house, still unsure of where should we start our new life. One day, Tomás said:

"It's time for our first plunge together! Those dreams we've talked about in Paris are waiting! And you know what they say: *Do not do to others what you would not want them to do to you.* You hate waiting!"

"What do you mean?"

"I mean it's time for us to buy a farm on Gold Coast, the place of a thousand beaches and countless sunny days. Last weekend when we were there, we both loved it. You'll start writing and I'll have my own restaurant. We'll be alright, mate!"

"Someone is fond of the Aussie slang! Deal! We'll paint it in tones of white and blue of the Argentinean flag and red and yellow of the Romanian one. I mean, the house, not the restaurant. The restaurant will be your place, you can paint it in whatever colors you like."

"The restaurant will be ours too, baby. Everything will be ours, not only mine. We'll adopt two Border Collie puppies, welcome a stray fluffy cat, get introduced to the cockatoo population and wait impatiently to see the whereabouts of the possums family living in our roof."

"I'll finally have my own veggie patch and a dozen books about how and when to grow everything that can be grown, including eatable weeds."

"Knowing you, now that your love affair with law is all done and dusted, that's all you'll study? Vegetables and eatable weeds?"

"I guess I could also study the types of chickens yielding the most number of eggs and how to distinguish a potent fierce rooster from a less endowed one. That will be fun! Next thing you'll know, I'll walk around the mall carrying a chicken in my arms, like Madam..."

"And her wild, crazy chicken, Loulou. But why not? Never say never. As long as you limit yourself to the study of the roosters' population is all fine with me."

"Even I have my limits, you know that."

"Yes, the sky!" he laughed.

And so it was. We moved.

When we entered our Mudgeeraba property, on Gold Coast, we felt a bit like the royal couple entering one of their vast luxurious domains. The only difference was no one was applauding us, we didn't have to wave graciously to every peasant smiling at us and there was no reception waiting at the end. A long winding driveway was showing us the way to a beautiful house surrounded by dense forest and palm trees.

"This is wonderful, Tomás! It's the whole aura of the place, contemplative, tranquil, yet so joyful," I said while my eyes were streaming with tears. This time, they were long due tears of happiness.

"It surely is. It's as we've already done our share of good deeds in this world. Hey, look, you made a friend already!" he pointed to the daring kookaburra right behind me.

"Isn't he something? They never come so close! We'll name him Fuzzy!"

And ever since that day, at four on the dot, Fuzzy came by, ready to be fed by hand with first quality beef mince. If I was late, he did not seem to mind, as long as I was coming well prepared.

I started to write each day about places, people and dreams, about the power of love and of our thoughts, about destiny, courage, resilience and confidence. For the first time in my life, I was doing something which I loved doing. It came naturally to me, it felt right, and it rewarded me each day with joy and hope.

I was not a famous lawyer, but an aspiring writer, a gardener with a chef by my side, traveling the world, having a small house, a big garden, some chicks and two loyal dogs to make it feel like home, and a fluffy cat to amuse us all.

And this made me happy. Because this was all that mattered.

After extraordinary adventures and high ambitions, I found happiness with a regular guy, forging a simple life and dreaming of simple pleasures.

I was finally at peace.

"Mom, this is a beautiful story!" Josephine, my first daughter said as soon as I closed the book.

"It is, my little princess. Now, the question is what will *you* do when the dreams are calling. Will you pick up?"

"I will. I will always pick up!"

Dear Reader, you might guess,
That I wish you all the best.
But before letting you go,
To face the usual ebb and flow,
I would like to say to you
That whatever you choose to do,
I hope you can always find
Strength, humor, and peace of mind!

Have you enjoyed this book? If so, why not write a review on your favourite website?

Thanks very much for buying my book.

Love,

Carol